*I dedicate this book to my wife, Stacey, and
my three children, Jed, Zoe and Max, because
it's their love that gave me the strength to do
this in the first place – H.W.*

*This book is for my four fabulous men –
Alan, Theo, Oliver and Cole. With love and
potato leek soup – L.O.*

CHAPTER 1

It started to buzz. I looked up. The loudspeaker above the door crackled and buzzed again. Then it started to shake. It was coming alive!

"Hank Zipzer!" the loudspeaker said. "Report to Mr Love's office at once."

I put my hands over my ears and slid down in my chair.

How did it know my name? It was only the first hour of the first day of school, and already my name was coming out of that box on the wall.

Everyone in class stared at me. Some kids giggled. A few of them whispered. But not Nick McKelty. Nope – he cupped his hands over his big mouth and shouted, "Way to go, Zipper Boy!"

My teacher, Ms Adolf, shot me a really nasty look.

Show no fear, I thought. *Walk the walk.*

HANK ZIPZER!

HANK ZIPZER

The WORLD'S GREATEST UNDERACHIEVER

and the CRAZY CLASSROOM CASCADE

HENRY WINKLER & LIN OLIVER

WALKER
BOOKS

First published in Great Britain as
Hank Zipzer the World's Greatest Underachiever: Niagara Falls – Or Does It? (2008)
by Walker Books Ltd, 87 Vauxhall Walk, London SE11 5HJ

First published in the United States as
Hank Zipzer #01: Niagara Falls – Or Does It? (2003) by Henry Winkler and Lin Oliver.
Published by arrangement with Grosset & Dunlap™, a division of Penguin Young Readers Group, a member of Penguin Group (USA) Inc. All rights reserved.

This edition published 2012

2 4 6 8 10 9 7 5 3 1

This book has been typeset in Sabon

Printed and bound in Great Britain by Clays Ltd, St Ives plc

British Library Cataloguing in Publication Data:
a catalogue record for this book is available from the British Library

ISBN 978-1-4063-4033-4

www.walker.co.uk

I stood up and strutted to the door like Shaquille O'Neal taking centre court. OK, so I wear a size-four shoe and he wears a size twenty-three – it's the attitude that matters. I'm big on attitude. Small on shoe but big on attitude.

When I reached the door, I turned to my best friend, Frankie Townsend. "If I don't come back," I told him, "you can have my protractor."

"Don't forget to breathe in there," Frankie whispered. "Remember, Zip, oxygen is power."

Frankie is very big on oxygen. Whenever I'm nervous, he always tells me to take some deep breaths. He learned that from his mum, who is a yoga teacher. She's really good at yoga. In fact, she's not good, she's great. She is so flexible, she can lift up her leg and put her foot in her pocket!

Even though I was going to the head teacher's office, I was determined to leave with style, my head held high. I flashed the class my best smile, the one where I show both my top and bottom teeth. Then, in the middle of maybe the greatest exit ever, the loudspeaker buzzed again.

"And don't you dare stop in the toilets, young man," it said.

Now how did it know I was going to do that?

Everyone laughed as I left.

"No laughing in class!" Ms Adolf shouted, banging on her desk with this pointer stick she has.

That's one of her rules. Ms Adolf doesn't believe in laughing. She thinks fourth-graders laugh way too much.

There are two fourth-grade teachers in my school. One is named Mr Sicilian, and he's really nice. He plays football with everyone at break time and never gives homework at the weekend. The other is Ms Adolf. She doesn't play any games and gives two tons of homework even on weekends. My luck, I got Ms Adolf.

I could practically hear my heart pounding as I walked down the corridor. Mr Love has a way of making you nervous, especially when you don't know what you've done wrong.

I was trying not to think about him, so I looked at all the "Welcome Back" decorations in the corridor instead. The corridors at my school are painted yuck green. You know, the colour of melted pistachio ice cream. But the decorations really helped to cheer things up. I liked Miss Hart's door, which had an underwater theme. All the fifth-graders in her class had pasted pictures of their faces on to octopus heads. Mr Sicilian's was my favourite. All the kids' heads were footballs. I told you he was cool.

When I reached the stairs, I thought about sliding down the banister, but I was already in enough trouble, so I took the stairs – two at a time. My mouth was dry when I got to the bottom, so I stopped at the water fountain to have a drink.

Just as I took the first gulp, the loudspeaker buzzed again.

"I'm waiting, Mr Zipzer," it said. Mr Love has the kind of voice that sounds like it belongs to a really tall man with a lot of bushy, black hair. But actually, Mr Love is short and bald except for a little fringe of red hair.

I ran down the corridor. I couldn't get into trouble for running in the corridors if the place I was running to was the head teacher's office, right?

When I got to the office, I took a deep breath. I looked up at the sign above the door. LELAND LOVE, HEAD TEACHER, it said. I had been here before. Many times. Too many times. Way, way, way too many times.

Slowly, I pushed open the door. I walked inside and came face to face with the five of them. No, not people – there was only one person there. I'm talking about *things*. The things on Mr Love's face: two eyes, two ears and one mole on his cheek that looked like the Statue of Liberty without the torch. I don't know if it's possible for a mole to frown, but trust me, this one did not look happy.

"Approach me, young man," Head Teacher Love said.

I wanted to, I really did, but my feet were stuck on his carpet. It was as if I had big wads of chewing gum stuck to the soles of my shoes.

"Were you or were you not late today?" Head Teacher Love asked.

I didn't answer because I've found that when Leland Love asks a question, he likes to answer it himself.

"You were seventeen minutes late," he said.

See what I mean?

"Did we not have this talk thirty times in third grade, fifteen times in second grade, and I won't even refer to first grade?" Mr Love's face twitched. It looked like the Statue of Liberty was doing a hula dance.

I tried not to laugh. That would have got me into even bigger trouble.

"We've had this talk many times," he answered himself. See, he did it again.

I looked down at my feet, mostly to stop myself from staring at the Statue of Liberty mole. Once you focus on that thing, it's really hard to take your eyes off it. I noticed that I had put on odd socks again. One had a Nike swoosh and the other was just your basic Walmart sock.

"If there's one thing I want you to learn from your experience at PS 87, it is this—" Mr Love was using his bushy-hair-tall-man voice. "Are you listening, young man?"

"I've got both ears working, sir."

Actually, I *was* listening. I really was curious to hear the single most important thing I was supposed to learn in my whole entire primary school career.

Head Teacher Love cleared his throat. "Always be on time, when time is involved," he said.

Wow. There it was. Now, if I could just figure out what it meant.

"Explain to me how it is possible that you were late on the very first day of school," he said.

OK, I'll be honest with you. I am late a lot, but I don't mean to be. In fact, I try really hard to have everything ready on time – my pencils all sharpened; my three ballpoint pens ready to roll; a protractor, a ruler *and* a compass in my pencil case. But this morning I had a problem. I'm pretty sure

I remember putting my rucksack on my desk chair before I went to bed. But somehow, and I don't have an exact reason for this, my rucksack played hide-and-seek during the night and this morning it took me twenty minutes to find it. It was in the cupboard by the front door. But try telling that to Leland Love.

"I'm waiting for an answer," said Head Teacher Love.

And all that squeaked out of me was, "Can't explain it, sir."

"Well then, absorb this," he said, "because I'm only going to say it once. Punctuality and the fourth grade go hand in hand." He paused, then said it again, just like I knew he would. "Punctuality and the fourth grade go hand in hand."

I'm not sure but I think the Statue of Liberty on his face nodded in agreement.

CHAPTER 2

I can't believe I'm saying this, but it was actually a relief to get back to Ms Adolf's class ... for about twenty seconds, anyway.

As soon as I slid into my chair, the words "Five full paragraphs are required" came flying out of Ms Adolf's mouth like heat-seeking missiles.

I looked around. All the other kids were writing in their homework books. I reached for my homework book too, but it was missing in action. I thought maybe I had left it in the middle drawer of my desk at home, underneath my broken watch collection. Or maybe on the kitchen table.

"The topic for your essay is: what I did in the summer holidays," Ms Adolf went on. As she wrote the words on the blackboard, I noticed that her skirt had lots of chalk marks in the butt region. That happens to teachers when they lean against the blackboard, but I had never seen chalk marks like this before. They looked like donkey ears. When I thought of Ms Adolf with a donkey on her bum, I couldn't help myself. I laughed out loud.

"Henry, I see nothing funny," Ms Adolf said. Of course she didn't. That's because she couldn't see her rear end.

I bit my lip and tried to concentrate.

"I expect you to write an opening paragraph, a concluding paragraph and three supporting paragraphs," Ms Adolf was saying.

I raised my hand.

"Exactly how long does a paragraph have to be?" I asked.

Everyone laughed, which was strange, because I wasn't trying to be funny. Ms Adolf didn't laugh. She got little red splotches on her neck, like the kind my sister, Emily, gets when she's really mad.

"Well, Henry," Ms Adolf said, saying my name

as if it smelled bad. "We will all learn that from you, since you'll be the first one to read your essay out loud to the class."

Ms Adolf walked to her desk. She wore a cord round her neck with a small key on it. The key was silver and so shiny that she must have polished it every night. She slipped the cord off and unlocked the top drawer of her desk with the key. I wondered what could be in there that had to be locked up. I looked at Frankie, who knew what I was thinking.

"Maybe she's got a big wad of cash in there," he whispered.

"Or jewels," said our friend Ashley Wong, who loves jewellery.

But when Ms Adolf opened the drawer, the only thing she took out was her register. She picked it up and started to write.

"Henry Zipzer, Monday at nine-fifteen," she said. "We will all look forward to hearing your essay then. Is that clear, Henry?"

"Ms Adolf," I said, "do you think you could call me Hank?"

"Why would I call you *Hank* when *Henry* is a perfectly fine name?" she said. She locked up her register and slipped the key back over her head.

"It's what my friends call me."

"Well, *I* am not your friend," Ms Adolf said. As if I hadn't already figured that out.

She reached down and picked a tiny piece of fluff off her skirt. I mean, it was so tiny you needed a microscope to see it. She held the bit of fluff in her hand and walked it carefully over to the bin. When she dropped it in, I'm telling you, I saw nothing leave her fingers.

I wondered why Ms Adolf would care so much about a piece of fluff. It's not like she looks that good anyway. All she ever wears are a grey skirt and a grey blouse, which match her grey hair and grey glasses, not to mention her grey face.

"Remember, class, that's *five* paragraphs," she said. "And neatness counts. I'll be expecting your very best work. That includes you, Henry."

Smile, Hank, I thought. *Nod your head, up and down. You can do this. Five paragraphs. What's the big deal? You've got six days.*

Oh come on, who am I kidding? I can't

even write *one* good sentence. So how am I ever going to write an entire five-paragraph essay? Ms Adolf might as well have asked me to ski down Mount Everest ... backwards ... blindfolded ... and butt naked.

CHAPTER 3

At lunch, I sat at the table and stared at my vegetarian bologna-sausage sandwich. Most of the other kids were waiting in the hot food queue. It was either macaroni cheese day or tuna-melt day. Or maybe it was both. I couldn't tell without looking at the menu, because all school food smells the same.

I looked around the dining room and spotted Frankie. He had just bought some milk and was laughing and talking with Katie Sperling and Kim Paulson, only the two most beautiful girls in the entire school. When Frankie smiles, he gets this huge dimple in his cheek. As he walked, he kept flashing the girls The Big Dimple. And, man, was it working! They were following him to our table. I couldn't believe it – Katie Sperling and Kim Paulson were going to sit down with us! That is, until Robert Upchurch cut in front of them and took the seat opposite me.

"Hey, Hank, mind if I sit here?" he asked.

"Yes," I answered, but it was too late.

When Katie and Kim saw Robert, they swerved left – at least I think it was left. Maybe it was right. It's hard for me to keep track of directions. Anyway, they went down a totally different aisle and sat with Ryan Shimozato and his friends. Robert isn't exactly a girl magnet. He has a neck the size of a pencil and always wears a starchy white shirt with a tie. (That's right, I said a *tie*.) Add to that the fact that he's the most boring person on the planet and you can't blame the girls for picking another table.

Frankie flopped down next to me. "Thanks, Robert," he said. "Nice work."

"What'd I do?" Robert asked. Poor kid, he really didn't have a clue.

Robert has just started third grade. Since the third-graders and fourth-graders at my school eat lunch together, this was the first day he'd had a chance to sit with us. We don't really want him hanging around with us, but he lives in the same block of flats as Frankie, Ashley and me, so he thinks he has the right to tag along everywhere.

Frankie glanced at my sandwich and made a face. He's been making faces at my lunches ever since we were in preschool.

"I see your mum's at it again," he said. "What's she calling this, soy surprise?"

"It's bologna," I told him.

"Bologna and I go *way* back," said Frankie, "and this is no bologna!"

I don't know if you've had vegetarian bologna before, but I don't think you've ever had my *mum's* vegetarian bologna. She thinks she invented it, which proves she should keep her thoughts to herself. My mum's vegetarian bologna tastes like nothing you've ever put in your mouth. Let's just say it's round, ground, pinkish leaves of grass. Let's just say it's non-food.

Ever since my mother took over Papa Pete's deli, she has been experimenting like crazy with food. Unfortunately for me, my lunch is her laboratory. Vegetarian bologna is only one of her experiments. You haven't lived until you've tried her soy salami. Papa Pete says it's a crime what she does to salami.

By the way, Papa Pete is my grandpa. He's the best. Sometimes I get the feeling that he's the only person who understands me. He never ever thinks I'm stupid or lazy.

"Actually, bologna is a very interesting word,"

Robert said through a mouthful of macaroni cheese.

Frankie and I looked at each other. You know how when you have a best friend, you and the other person often think the same thing at the same time? We were both thinking, *Somebody get me out of this conversation!*

"What's especially interesting is that bologna contains a silent *g*, just like the silent *k* in *knock* or *knight*," Robert went on.

Robert knows everything. That's why he skipped second grade. I think it's great to know a lot of things. I just don't think you have to say them all the time. Like Robert will name all the James Bond movies in order, including the year they came out, even when no one asks him. And don't even start him on world capitals. He'll tell you the capital of Indonesia right in the middle of a dodgeball game. The other day he just looked at me and said, "The human body has enough iron to make one nail." He said it like it was a totally normal thing to say!

"Robert," I said, "why don't you go and sit with the third-graders."

"They're not interested in what I have to say," he said.

"We're not interested either," I said.

"Why not?" he answered. "Spelling is a very challenging subject."

"Challenging?" I said. "That's the understatement of the century. I can't spell to save my life. And it really bothers me too."

"I can't imagine not being able to spell," Robert said. "Doesn't it make you feel stupid?"

"Robert, will you give Zip a break?" said Frankie, giving him a noogie on the head. "Can't you see he's a troubled man?"

"What's wrong with you?" Robert asked.

"Ms Adolf is making us write an entire five-paragraph essay," I answered. "Neatness counts. Punctuation counts. Everything counts. Do you realize how impossible that is?"

Just then, Ashley slid on to the bench next to me and put her tray down. She had chosen both the macaroni cheese and the tuna-melt. Ashley likes variety – in everything. You should see her clothes. She covers them all with rhinestones – even her trainers. She's got one pair with a family of dolphins swimming in the ocean, in blue and green rhinestones. She glues them all on herself.

"What's impossible?" asked Ashley.

"Spelling," I said.

"Spelling is hard," she agreed.

"But this is impossible."

She picked up a cherry that was sitting on top of her fruit salad. She popped it into her mouth and ate it. Then her face got all twisted up and busy, like a chipmunk shelling an acorn. In no time, she stuck out her tongue and there was the cherry stem, tied in a perfect knot. Is Ashley Wong an amazing girl or what?

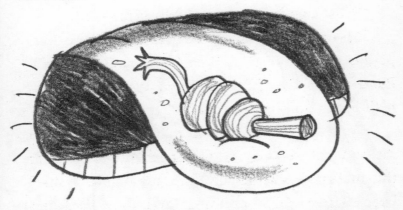

"Ashweena, that is so cool," said Frankie. Frankie has a nickname for everyone. He even calls my dad Mr Z. No one else I know even *talks* to my father.

"Does nobody care about my problem?" I said. "Is anybody listening?"

My friends stopped eating and looked at me.

"How am I going to write five perfect paragraphs by next Monday when I can't get what I'm thinking about down on paper?" I said. "My handwriting looks like a chicken stepped in tar and ran across the page."

"If a chicken stepped in tar, it would get stuck and couldn't run anywhere," Robert pointed out.

"Shut up, Robert," we all said together.

"I put commas in the wrong places," I continued. "My capital letters look weird. My lowercase letters look even weirder. My spelling – well, we all know about my spelling."

"Take a breath, Zip," said Frankie. "We'll figure it out. Hey, make friends with the dictionary. Let your fingers do the walking, if you know what I'm talking about."

Frankie is really good at school. He thinks maths is easy *and* get this – he reads for fun. I wish I could do that. I wish it was easier for me to read a book.

"You sound just like my father," I said. "He's always telling me to look up words in the dictionary."

Suddenly, Frankie grabbed his chest and fell to the ground, flopping around like he was some kind of alien. He's cool enough to be able to do a thing like that in the dining room. Even Katie Sperling and Kim Paulson were laughing. Not at him, either, but with him.

"That hurts!" he screamed. "Comparing me to Silent Stan, the crossword-puzzle man." (That's another one of Frankie's nicknames for my dad.)

Frankie got up and sat back down at the table. "Someone, please. What's a four-letter word for a root vegetable?" he said, doing a perfect imitation of my father working on a crossword puzzle.

We all cracked up. Milk came shooting out of Ashley's nose. It splattered all over her T-shirt, spraying the rhinestone self-portrait she had done. Drops of milk hung off the purple stones she had used for the frames of her glasses.

"Does anyone have a napkin?" she asked.

"Here, take mine," I told her. "My sandwich is never going to make it to my mouth anyway."

"Do me a favour, Zip," Frankie said. "Don't ever tell me that I sound like your father again."

"Then don't bring up the dictionary again," I said. "It's such a useless invention. At least for me."

"Don't tell that to Ms Adolf," said Ashley. "She's in love with dictionaries."

"They don't make any sense," I said. "I can't spell words because I can't sound them out. So how am I going to find them in a dictionary if I can't spell them in the first place? Do you know my dictionary has one thousand two hundred and fifty-six pages? Words get lost in there."

"Zip, you're forgetting to…"

"… breathe. I know, Frankie. I *am* breathing."

Frankie put his hand on my shoulder. "Look, it's just an essay, my man."

"Maybe for you," I said. "For me, it's torture."

Frankie reached into his lunchbox and pulled out a packet of Ding Dongs. He took one for himself and gave one to me.

"Listen up, Zip," he said. "We're supposed to write about what we did in our summer holidays, right? So just write about what happened to you. You had an awesome summer holiday – going to Canada and to Niagara Falls and getting to steer the boat all by yourself when the captain fell overboard. Man, that's cool stuff."

Ashley nearly choked on her second cherry stem.

"That's not what you told *me*," she said. "You told me your sister got seasick and threw up all over your plastic raincoat."

OK, OK, so sometimes I tell stories. But

they're not lies or anything. It's just that I think the world needs to be entertained. I happen to be good at it. Like Papa Pete says, "If you got it, flaunt it." Flaunt. There's another word I can't spell.

Suddenly, out of nowhere came a hand bigger than an average hand. Bigger than a tabletop. Then a head the size of Rhode Island appeared. Next came the smell of bad, bad breath – the kind that makes the gel in your hair lose its grip.

"That Ding Dong is mine," Nick McKelty said as he smashed what was once my chocolate bar into his oversized mouth. "I wuffofv deese."

Robert dived for cover under the table. Ashley shot milk again.

"Be my guest," I said. It was either that or have Nick the Tick pound my skull with his knuckles. Nick thinks that because he is the biggest guy in the fourth grade, everybody's lunch is his personal meal. We are his menu and he just takes whatever he wants.

Nick was looking for his second course. My instincts told me he was headed for Ashley's tuna-melt.

"Nick!" I said, yelling to catch his attention. "You don't want to eat that."

"Like you're going to stop me," he said, flashing me his stupid grin. The Ding Dong chocolate was wedged in the gap between his teeth so it looked like he had three front teeth.

"Did you hear about the tuna they just caught off Cape Cod that ate a licence plate from a car from Ohio?" I said to him, thinking fast. "There was so much metal ground up inside him that by the time he got to the shop he didn't need a tin."

I pointed to Ashley's sandwich. "That's him in there."

You could almost hear the small wheels grinding inside his huge blond head.

"I didn't want that pathetic sandwich anyway," he said. "I've got to save my appetite for the Knicks' basketball game tonight. My dad's got tickets for right next to the players' bench."

Nick's father owns the local bowling alley, McKelty's Roll 'N Bowl. Maybe that's why Nick the Tick thinks he has the right to act like a big shot all the time. All he does is brag, and none of it is ever true.

OK, like I said before, I tell stories sometimes too. But let's get one thing straight: my stories are purely for entertainment purposes. Nick's stories are to make him seem cool. Which he's not, I might add. Like, he says his father has the best seats for every sporting event in the United States of America. The truth is, they mostly watch the games on the TV at the bowling alley. That's what we call The McKelty Factor. Truth times a hundred.

In any case, Nick walked away. Ashley smiled at me. "Thanks, Hank," she said.

I felt proud. I had saved her lunch.

"You are amazing, Zip," Frankie said. "You have so much trouble with so many things, but never with your mouth. It's a brilliant mouth."

I thought about that. If my brilliant mouth worked on Nick McKelty, why couldn't it work on Ms Adolf?

I took out a piece of paper and a pencil. I had a plan.

CHAPTER 4

Before lunch ended, I decided to find Ms Adolf and have a little chat. She was sitting at her desk, finishing her lunch. Two big napkins covered most of her. Just her shoes were showing. They were grey. She was eating a banana that was so brown you couldn't even tell it had ever been yellow.

"May I talk to you for a minute, Ms Adolf?" I asked from the doorway.

She waved me inside.

"I've been thinking a lot about my essay," I began.

"I'm glad to hear that, Henry," she said.

"What I've been thinking about, exactly, is that it would really benefit you if I don't write this essay."

"Is that so?" she said. She tossed the banana skin into the bin.

"In fact, I've spent a good part of my lunch break writing a list of ten really excellent reasons why I shouldn't write this essay."

I pulled the piece of paper from my back pocket and flattened it out on her desk with the palm of my hand. There was a big, greasy smudge on it. And it really, really smelled like tuna fish. I have to admit it was pretty disgusting.

"Sorry," I said, trying to rub it off. "It was tuna-melt day. Just pretend it's a scratch-and-sniff."

I smiled. Ms Adolf didn't.

That wasn't a good start, but I had to think positively. I stood very quietly while she read the list.

TEN REASONS WHY HANK ZIPZER SHOULD NOT WRITE A FIVE-PARAGRAPH ESSAY ON "WHAT I DID THIS SUMMER"

1. Every pen I own runs out of ink.
2. My thoughts are controlled by alien beings who make me write in a strange language.
3. We couldn't go anywhere over the summer because my dog had a nervous breakdown.
4. I'm highly allergic to lined paper.
5. When I write, my fingers stick together.
6. If I sit too long, my bum falls asleep and snores, which keeps my sister awake.
7. Every time I write an essay, my dog Cheerio eats it for breakfast before I can get to school. So why try?
8. My computer keyboard is missing eleven letters — v, c, t, s, m and all the vowels including y and w.
9.
10.

The last two reasons were on the tip of my tongue, but I just couldn't get them to the tip of my pencil.

Ms Adolf put down the list and looked up at me. "This is very creative," she said.

Creative. Creative is good. My plan was working.

"I hope you'll use some of this creativity in your essay," she went on. "I look forward to hearing you read your written words on Monday morning."

Then she took my list, crumpled it up and tossed it in the bin. *There is my creativity,* I thought – *stuck to the top of a brown banana skin.*

CHAPTER 5

Three, two, one. Brrriinnngg. The bell. After an endless afternoon of alphabetizing practice, the first day of fourth grade was finally over. Frankie and I looked at each other. We were free men.

Frankie, Ashley and I ran downstairs and practically flew out the front door of the school building. Papa Pete was waiting outside to walk us home. He was helping Mr Baker, the lollipop man, take the little kids across the road. Papa Pete is my mother's father. He also happens to be one of the greatest human beings on the face of the earth.

"There he is," said Frankie, waving to Papa

Pete. "Get your cheeks ready."

When Papa Pete sees you, he gives you a big pinch and says, "I love this cheek and everything that's attached to it." I know this sounds like it's annoying, but actually it makes you feel really good.

Papa Pete gave us each a pinch and a hug. "I hardly recognized you kids," he said. "You look so much older now that you're in the fourth grade."

We had hoped that this would be the year we'd be allowed to walk home from school by ourselves. After all, Frankie, Ashley and I lived in the same block of flats, so we could all walk together. Safety in numbers, we all told our parents. But we were all turned down flat. New York City is not a place for kids to be wandering around alone, our parents said.

OK, we could live with that, because having Papa Pete walk you home is actually pretty fun. He walks a few metres behind us to make it *look* like we're walking alone. Papa Pete is so big that there is no way we could lose him in a crowd, even if we tried. It's not that he's tall, he's just large, the way a grizzly bear is large. My Grandma Jennie used to call him her big, cuddly grizzly bear. Maybe that was because he also has a ton of curly black hair on his arms and a huge moustache he calls his handlebars. After he eats something messy, he'll always say, "Tell me, Hank. Do I have anything hanging off the old handlebars?" I always tell him if he does, because he doesn't want to be embarrassed.

We headed up Amsterdam Avenue. We walked a couple of blocks and passed Harvey's, our favourite pizza place. It's no wider than a corridor, but they have the greatest Cherry Cokes and pizza there. You can smell it blocks away.

"I say we stop in for a slice," Frankie said.

Papa Pete shook his head. "Hold on, partner. We've got bigger bread to butter."

When Papa Pete says a thing like that, you don't argue. He's always got something great waiting for you.

We passed the man on the corner selling sunglasses. "Hey, gentlemen and lady," he said to us. "I've got a special pair just for your face."

Ashley stopped to look at a pair of rhinestone-covered glasses, but Frankie and I pulled her away. You can't let Ashley get started on rhinestones or you'll be there all day. She's a complete rhinestone nut.

Messengers on motorbikes whizzed by us. Mums coming back from the park pushed their babies in buggies. I love to see the babies' feet hanging out of the buggies. It always amazes me that inside their little bitty feet are big feet waiting to pop out and play baseball.

A couple of blocks up, we passed my mum's deli, the one Papa Pete started. It's called The Crunchy Pickle. They serve sandwiches so high they have to be held together with a toothpick. I waved at Carlos, who works behind the counter. I could see him shouting something, and even though I couldn't hear him, I knew he was saying, "Hey, Little Man."

"Hey, Big Man," I called back.

When we got to our block of flats, Frankie and Ashley started to go inside. Papa Pete steered them back on to the pavement.

"You haven't forgotten, have you?" he said.

"We have some business to conduct. I was thinking maybe you could come to my office."

Papa Pete's "office" is McKelty's Roll 'N Bowl. It's his hangout, his home from home. Everyone there knows him. He's the best senior bowler on the Upper West Side of Manhattan.

"I'll have to ask my parents," Ashley said.

"I took the liberty of phoning the good Doctors Wong," said Papa Pete, "and they said you don't have to be home until six." Although Ashley's parents are both doctors, Papa Pete is the only one I know who calls them "the good Doctors Wong". They don't seem to mind, though.

"I don't think my mum will let me go," Frankie said. "My dad teaches tonight and she likes me home."

Frankie's dad teaches African-American studies at Columbia University, which is thirty-eight blocks uptown. Once, his dad let me go to one of his lectures. He talked for almost two hours. I don't think I'll ever go to university if you have to sit still and listen to someone talk for two hours – and take notes at the same time.

"Fortunately for you, your mother was standing

43

on her head when I called," Papa Pete said to Frankie, "so I spoke to your father. When I explained that we were discussing important business, he said OK."

That was all we needed to hear. We took off for McKelty's, which is only a couple of blocks from our building. It's located on the second floor above the ninety-nine-cent shop, where I do most of my present buying. I bought my mum some earrings there for Mother's Day. She doesn't wear them much, though, because they hurt her lobes. Lots of people who shop at the ninety-nine-cent shop don't even realize that there's a bowling alley upstairs. You can hardly see it from the street, but it's got fifteen lanes, video games and a coffee shop, too.

When we got to McKelty's, the lanes were full of Papa Pete's friends. They were all wearing their different coloured team shirts. They waved at us as we took a seat in one of the red plastic booths in the coffee shop.

"Fern!" Papa Pete called out. "Three root-beer floats for my grandkids here."

The fact that Frankie is African-American and Ashley's parents are from Taiwan doesn't stop Papa Pete from calling them his grandkids. That's another thing I love about him. And another is that he'll always buy you as many root beer floats as you want without ever mentioning that they will spoil your appetite for dinner.

Fern, who has been working at McKelty's for like a hundred and fifty years, brought us our root-beer floats.

As we were slurping down the last of our ice cream, Papa Pete started talking. "OK, let's get down to business," he said, wiping some whipped cream from his moustache. "I believe you've got a little something to show me."

I haven't mentioned this before, because sometimes I forget things, but Frankie is an outrageous magician. He doesn't just do the tricks you can buy in the shops, either. He makes up his own. Anybody can make a nickel disappear and then pull it out of your ear. But Frankie can make a *quarter* disappear and then have five nickels drop out of his nose. Now *that's* what I call *magic*.

Papa Pete was thinking of hiring him to be the entertainment at his Bowling League's Start of the Season Party. His team is called The Chopped

Livers. Everything about Papa Pete has to do with the deli he used to own – like his two parakeets are named Lox and Bagels. I'm surprised he didn't name my mother Pickled Herring.

"Let's see what you can do," Papa Pete said to Frankie.

"You mean you're making the kid audition?" Fern said.

"Business is business," answered Papa Pete, winking at Ashley and pinching my cheek, all at the same time.

Frankie reached into his rucksack, got out three red cups and placed them in a row on the table.

"What you see before you are three ordinary red cups," he began. He took out two small- and one medium-sized royal blue sponge balls that he mushed together into the palm of his hand. He asked Ashley to blow on his closed hand three times, then opened his palm and the balls had transformed into one big blue sponge ball. He put that ball under the middle red cup. He moved all the cups around in a flurry, then put them in a stack.

"*Zengawii!*" chanted Frankie. It's a word he made up when he went to Zimbabwe with his parents a couple of years ago. Frankie says it has magical powers.

He lifted the stack of cups high in the air. There on the table were two small- and one medium-sized sponge balls.

ZENGAWII!

"You're hired," Papa Pete said, applauding. "Do you want the job?"

"Could I have a word with my associates for a moment?" I asked Papa Pete. "In private."

I pulled Frankie and Ashley off to the side.

47

"I see a future here for us all," I said. "Frankie, you're the head magician, but you're going to need an assistant, which is me. And we'll need a business manager. That's you, Ashley. You'll make us millionaires."

"I want to be an assistant, too," Ashley said.

"OK," I said. "We'll take turns. But you still have to be the money person, because I'm dangerous with numbers." Last week, I went to buy a slice of pizza and they were out of dollar bills, so the guy gave me change all in coins. I just had to trust that he had given me the right change, because there was no way I could add it all up in my head. I would have needed a pad of paper, a pencil and my sister, Emily, who is like a human calculator, to figure it out.

"OK," said Ashley. "Since I'm the business person, let me do the talking."

"Go for it, Ashweena," said Frankie, slapping her a high five.

We went back over to Papa Pete.

"In the last few minutes, we've formed a partnership," said Ashley. "We've considered your offer, and my partners and I believe that for seventy-five dollars, we can put on a magic show that will never be forgotten."

"I believe," said Papa Pete, tugging on his moustache, "that for *thirty* dollars, you can put on a magic show that I'll like even better."

"Take it," I whispered in Ashley's ear. "It'll only go down from here."

"Deal," Ashley said. And she stuck out her hand.

Papa Pete shook it and said, "And of course, for this kind of money, I'd hope to see a small live furry thing coming out of a top hat. I always enjoy that."

"No problem," Ashley said.

Frankie and I shot each other panicked looks. Why was she promising that? We didn't have a small live furry thing.

We grabbed Ashley by the arm and pulled her over to the video game room. I knew I had to get her away from Papa Pete before she agreed to make the Empire State Building disappear.

"What were you thinking?" I said to Ashley.

"I was thinking about a rabbit," she said. "It's

always nice to pull a rabbit out of a hat."

"Earth to Ashley," said Frankie. "We don't have a rabbit."

"That's a good point," she said.

"Now what are we going to do?" I asked. "You promised Papa Pete we'd pull a live furry thing out of a top hat! He's counting on it."

Ashley just smiled. "You'll think of something, Hank. You always do."

CHAPTER 6

On the walk home, we couldn't stop coming up
with names for our new magic business. When we
left McKelty's, we thought The Magic Trio
sounded really good. Smooth and simple. By the
time we crossed the road, we had switched to
something flashier, like The Three Magicteers.
When we saw a neon sign in front of the all-night
laundrette, we came up with Magic: Open All Night.
By 83rd Street, Frankie was convinced we should
be The Mystical Magical Dudes. By 82nd Street,
Ashley was pushing for The Disappearing Act.

By the time we reached 78th street, we had
decided. We were Magik 3. Frankie thought we

should definitely spell Magic with a *k* because it looks cool. That was fine with me, since that's the way I thought it was spelled anyway.

It felt so great to have a name. And a plan. We figured we'd start our career at McKelty's Roll 'N Bowl. Then we'd move on to kids' parties and become known all over the entire West Side. Next, we'd take our show downtown. And finally on to Madison Square Garden where there'd be thousands of fans, chanting our name: "Magik 3! Magik 3! Magik 3!"

We decided to start rehearsals right away, so we scheduled a kick-off meeting for right after dinner. I was so excited about Magik 3 that I couldn't wait to go upstairs and tell my parents about us. I buzzed our flat number. My sister, Emily, answered the intercom.

"Who's there?" she asked.

"Open sesame," I said in my magician assistant's voice.

"Hank? Is that you? Why do you sound so weird?"

"The Mighty Zengawii requests that you let him in ... in ... in..." I gave my voice this really cool echo. Frankie and Ashley cracked up.

"Mum!" Emily yelled. "Hank's downstairs and he thinks he's being funny but he's not."

"Just buzz him in, honey," I heard my mum say over the sound of the blender in the kitchen.

"I'm letting you in," Emily said. "But if it were up to me, I'd leave you standing down there until you acted normal."

That's a strange thing to say coming from Emily, who's about as *un*normal as a person can be.

Frankie, Ashley and I got into the lift and pressed for our floors. I live on ten, which is the top floor. Frankie lives on six and Ashley lives on four. As we rode up, I imagined the three of us dressed in black capes and top hats. We'd all have moustaches. Ashley would look so funny in a moustache. The lift stopped at her floor. I pushed the door open and held it with my foot. We all put our hands out and placed them on top of one another's.

"Magik 3 rules," we chanted.

Ashley got out. Frankie and I headed for six.

"Watch this," said Frankie. He snapped his fingers and said, "Zengawii." The lift stopped and the door opened on his floor.

I rode by myself up to ten. When I got out, I shoved my key into the lock and made my entrance into the flat.

"Good evening, ladies and gentlemen of the Zipzer family," I said, with a sweep of my imaginary cape. "Welcome to the most astounding show you will ever behold, featuring the amazing talents of Magik 3! I am one of them."

I took a bow.

No one said a word.

My dog, Cheerio, ran up to me to say hello. At least someone in the family appreciated me. I took another bow. A really deep one. A really long one.

"I'm going to my room until dinner," Emily said. "This is too strange for me."

My father was sitting in his boxers at the dining-room table, working on a crossword puzzle. He was wearing a pair of glasses on the top of his head. He does that sometimes, even though I'm pretty sure he doesn't have eyes up there. He looked at me like I was a short stranger.

"You're late," he said.

"We were with Papa Pete at McKelty's."

"You should have called."

"But I was with Papa Pete. Not some stranger," I told him.

"You have to learn to be responsible, Hank," he answered back.

Responsible? I'm a small-business owner. How much more responsible can you get? But I didn't tell my dad that.

"I'm sorry, Dad," I said. "I'll call next time."

My mother came in from the kitchen. I could tell she'd been cooking because her hair was pulled back with a hairband. Her hair is blonde and curly, and when she wears it loose, bits of the food she's cooking sometimes land in it. She's had all kinds of things in her hair – flour, chunks of chocolate-chip-cookie dough. Once, she even found a bean. The hairband is her new discovery, and it's been working really well for her.

Mum started to push my father's papers to the end of the dining-room table. We eat at one end of the table and his office is at the other. He does something with computers. I'm not sure what it is, but I know it's pretty boring.

"How was your first day, my big fourth-grader?" my mum asked, kissing me on the cheek. "Did you remember to bring home your homework sheet?"

"That would be a first," said Emily the Perfect. She came out of her bedroom carrying her iguana, Katherine, on her shoulder. Who names a lizard Katherine?

Some people say that Emily and I look alike. Even though she's fifteen months younger than me, we're almost the same size. We both have blue eyes and blond hair that goes in a lot of different directions, like my dad's. But as far as I'm concerned, that's where the similarity ends. For one thing, I don't paint each fingernail a different colour like Emily does. And for another, I don't have to use Chapstick all the time because I lick my lips too much. And most importantly, I don't walk around with an iguana on my shoulder.

My sister Emily calls herself a reptile person. I call her a *creepy* reptile person. I mean, you're trying to enjoy your dinner and all of a sudden, her iguana snaps its long tongue out and snatches a carrot off your plate. How can a guy digest? And my parents don't say anything. Not a word!

My mum went back to the kitchen and brought out some soup for dinner. It was mushroom. I could tell it was Papa Pete's recipe because it smelled great. She served everyone up a big bowl, took off her hairband and apron, and sat down at the table.

"Who wants to share their day?" Mum asked. She says this every night at dinner. The great thing is that she really wants to hear all about your day.

I let Emily start.

"Who do you think got appointed rubber monitor?" she said. "Me. And our teacher, Miss Springflower, said I have the neatest handwriting she's ever seen. And she was really impressed with my summer reading list. She said she's never met a not-even third-grader who could read a three hundred and twenty-nine page book. I think I'm her favourite, and it's only the first day."

The only thought that came to my mind was, *Could you barf?*

The iguana's elastic tongue shot out for some soup. She missed, and her tongue made the soup splash high out of the bowl, hitting my father smack in the eye.

"Emily, take that thing and put it back in your room," he said.

Finally, he was reacting in a normal way.

"This so-called thing is an iguana whose natural habitat is the Galapagos," Emily said.

"So, can we FedEx it back home?" I asked.

My father chuckled.

"Stanley," said Mum. "Katherine is a member of this family, too."

"And what am I?" said my dad. "A lowly fly on the wall?"

I love it when adults say things like that – things that sort of make sense but don't really.

"Let's not spoil a nice dinner," said my mum. She turned her attention to me. I was crumbling a cracker into my soup. I like to float the pieces, watch them get soggy and eat them just before they sink.

"Hank," said my mum. "It's your turn. Let's hear about your day."

"My teacher, Ms Adolf, is so strict," I began. "We have to write a *huge* essay about what we did in our summer holidays. Five paragraphs."

No sooner were the words out of my mouth than I knew I had made a big mistake. My father wanted to know when it was due. My mother wanted to know when I was planning to start. Knowing me, they both suggested I begin tonight.

"I want to start on it, because you know how much I believe in getting an early start on things," I said with my fingers crossed. "But tonight I have a very important meeting in the clubhouse at seven."

"Honey, you know how long it takes you to do your homework," said my mother.

"This is the first homework assignment of the year," added my father. "You have to make a good impression on your teacher."

"But my business partners are counting on me," I pleaded.

"What business partners?" my father asked, getting irritated.

"Now, Henry…" my mother said.

Uh-oh. The H-word. Whenever she calls me Henry, I know it's all over.

"We've talked about starting this school year off on the right foot. I know you want to do that, don't you?"

"But I have six whole days to write it," I said. "That's less than a paragraph a day. And this meeting could change my entire life. And yours."

"That's enough," my father said. "Right after dessert, you're going to march into your room, sit down at your desk and start writing. I want one paragraph completed tonight."

Just then, Katherine flipped out her disgusting tongue and snapped up the last piece of cracker that I'd been saving.

This night was going nowhere fast.

CHAPTER 7

I love my room and I hate my room.

My bunk bed can be turned into a fort. All I have to do is tuck the blankets under the top mattress and let them hang down to the floor. I sleep on the bottom bunk and my desk is directly opposite the window. Everything is where I want it to be. My clock radio is by my bed. My CD player is portable, so it can move to where I need it. Inside my cupboard I have a secret panel where an old cigar box holds the most important items on Earth. There's a dollar note that Mum gave me for helping to clean up our dog's poo, a red star that my first-grade teacher gave me for telling the best story, my very first Hot Wheels car – a silver Ferrari F-50 convertible that I named Shiny – a load of baseball cards that will be very valuable someday and … that's pretty much it.

Those are the things I love about my room. What I hate about my room is that's where homework calls to me day and night like a monster. "Finish me. Finish me. Pick up your pencil."

I sat down at my desk and took out a piece of lined paper. Let's not forget that I'm allergic to lined paper. But I was determined to concentrate and get some of my essay done.

Cheerio ran into my room. He started to spin round in a circle. Now let me ask you this: how can a guy concentrate when his dog spends most of his waking hours chasing his tail? Cheerio, who is a very long dachshund, has been trying to catch his tail since he was a puppy. That's how he got his name. He's beigeish-brownish. So is a Cheerio. He looks like a circle. So does a Cheerio. Sometimes he spills his milk on himself, and then he looks like a *bowl* of Cheerios.

Watching Cheerio spin is like watching clothes twirling around in the dryer. It's boring, and you try to look away. But somehow you're just sucked in.

I was finally able to unhook my eyes from Cheerio and look at my desk. The lined paper stared up at me. My pencil was sharpened and ready. So why couldn't I just pick it up and write ... something ... anything? The piece of paper looked like it was spinning around the desktop ... like my dog. I pushed my hand straight out to stop it. My thoughts were spinning. *Niagara Falls*... I wrote that down. At last, something was coming. *My family is in raincoats and boots and rain hats. We had to rent them.* I wrote that down, too.

All of a sudden, I looked down and saw that my desk drawer was open a crack. My hand just shot down and pulled it open even further. Boy, was it a mess! How did that happen? I felt this powerful need to straighten up everything in my drawer.

My broken watch collection was all over the place. My special marbles had rolled all the way to the back. I took some Scotch tape and taped the marbles down. I was on fire! Then I noticed that the ballpoint pens had somehow got into the pencil part of the divider. I couldn't have that.

"Henry Zipzer, are you writing your essay?" my mother called from outside my door.

I slammed the drawer shut and picked up my pencil.

"You bet, Mum."

I looked down at the paper. I squinted and saw a sentence and a half – that was all I had written. I looked at my clock radio. We had a seven o'clock meeting in our clubhouse down in the basement. How was I going to make it? I'd never get out of my room. I hated my room. I hated my essay. I hated my brain. Why couldn't I think or write or spell or add or divide? Forget about multiplying.

It's not like I don't try. I do. I go over and over and over my times tables and my vocabulary lists. My sister tests me, and I know everything. But then comes the test, and I can't remember them. It's like my mind is a blackboard and the words just slide off it in the time it takes to walk from my flat to school, which is a block and a half away. It makes me so mad that sometimes I hit my head with my fist, hoping I'll start everything working again.

The piece of paper was still there in front of me. Still pretty much empty. I picked up my pencil and reread my sentence and a half. Great. I had spelled Niagara wrong. Rubbing out was a trick.

My rubber usually ripped the paper to shreds. As I moved it over the sheet of paper, a hole started to appear. Small at first, and then it grew. It finally got so big, I could see the desktop through it.

I screwed up the sheet of paper and threw it. It hit the rim of my bin. Mum and Dad gave the bin to me for my birthday last year, and they put family pictures all around the outside under plastic.

Start again, Hank, I told myself. *Think.* Niagara Falls ... or Does It? *by Hank Zipzer.*

I wondered if the title could be considered a paragraph?

Probably not.

CHAPTER 8

"**Man, are you late!**" Frankie said, a little bit angrily. "It's seven-thirty."

"We thought you weren't coming," Ashley chimed in.

"Hey, *I* didn't think I was coming," I snapped back. "Parent problems."

"I happen to know that your mum isn't even home," said Frankie. "I know that because she's upside-down in my living room."

"My dad went to yoga class tonight too," said Ashley. "He said he needed to de-stress. I'd be stressed too if I had to look at pictures of people's disgusting insides all day."

"We've got to get my dad to go to yoga," I said. "He could definitely use some de-stressing. He wouldn't let me come here tonight until I had written a paragraph of my essay."

"Did you do one?" asked Ashley.

"Yeah, I wrote a paragraph."

"Great," said Ashley, throwing an arm round me.

"Then I rubbed it out."

"Not so great." Ashley looked worried.

"I assume you didn't mention the rubbing out part to Silent Stan," said Frankie.

"He didn't ask, and I didn't tell."

I don't lie to my parents, but I have to confess, there are times when I don't tell them everything. I think you know what I mean.

I fell backwards into one of the sofas that lined the wall of our clubhouse. Cheerio, who had come with me, started to sniff the place out. He always sniffs around like he's going to find something new. He never does, but as long as he doesn't lift his leg, I figure he can do whatever he wants.

Our clubhouse is in the basement of our block of flats. When you get out of the lift, you start smelling soapsuds because the laundry room is to the right. But if you turn to the left, there are three rooms with padlocks on them filled with stuff no one in the building wants. Old chairs and sofas and bird cages, suitcases of every size, boxes of books and food magazines. A lot of parent kind of stuff.

One of the rooms doesn't have a lock so we use it for our hideout. It's a perfect meeting spot. Well, almost perfect. It would be totally perfect if Robert didn't know about it.

Ashley and Frankie had already made a list of the tricks Frankie was going to do for Papa Pete's show. It said:

1. Take nickels from nose.
2. Transform one scarf into many scarves.
3. Make thumb disappear.
4. Pull live furry thing from hat.

"Numbers one to three are no-brainers," Frankie said, "but number four isn't going to happen. We'd better face it now."

"But I promised Papa Pete," said Ashley. "I shook on it."

"Fine," said Frankie. "Then you've got to find me something live and furry."

"How about Robert?" I suggested.

"No," said Frankie. "His mother would freak out if we tried to stuff him in a hat."

Cheerio got tired of sniffing and started to chase his tail.

"Cheerio's at it again," Ashley said. "Doesn't he ever get dizzy?"

I looked at Cheerio twirling around like a top. A flash of inspiration hit me. Cheerio! He was small. He was furry. He was alive.

"Members of Magik 3," I said as I sprang off the sofa. "I have the answer. We're pulling Cheerio out of that hat."

When he heard his name, Cheerio stopped spinning for a minute and looked me right in the eye. Then he started spinning again.

Frankie put his hand to his forehead, like he had a bad headache. "He does that inside a hat and I'm telling you right now, he'll burn a hole in the fabric."

"Cheerio can be calm," I said. "He'll co-operate."

"Right, and my name is Bernice," said Frankie. "By the way, here's another question, guys. What top hat have you ever seen that this dog would fit in?"

"He's our best choice, Frankie. He's also our *only* choice," Ashley said. "So we'll just have to figure out a way." She pushed her glasses up on her nose and folded her arms in a way that meant business.

Ashley can be tough when she wants to be.

"I think we can build a hat big enough to hold Cheerio," I suggested. "There's stuff all over here that we could use."

"Yeah, like what?" Frankie asked.

I looked around. On the shelf above the door, I saw a big, round hatbox kind of thing. We pulled it down, took off the lid and put Cheerio inside. He fitted perfectly.

"Great, we'll use this," I said. "We'll cover it in black felt."

"Like we happen to have a big pile of felt lying around," Frankie said.

"I know where they sell felt." I had just seen some the week before in the ninety-nine-cent shop. It was in the school supplies section.

"It's still not going to look like a hat," said Frankie.

"Then we'll get some cardboard and make a brim," I answered.

"That sounds hard," said Ashley. "How will we get the brim to stick on?"

"Trust me," I said. "I'm a genius with super glue."

"OK, genius," said Frankie, "tell me how we're going to keep your nutcase dog inside the hat until it's time to pull him out?"

"I'll build a pocket inside and put some biscuits there to keep Cheerio calm." By now, Frankie and Ashley were pretty impressed with my ideas. I have to admit, I was too.

"We can even put the whole hat on wheels," I said. I don't know where that idea came from. It just popped into my mind. One second there was nothing in my head, and the next second there was a hat on wheels. It was amazing.

"Hank, you are covered in creativity," Ashley said.

"You're the second person today who's used that word," I said to her. "Ms Adolf told me she was looking forward to seeing me use my creativity in my essay."

Then it struck me. Creativity. It was the answer to all my problems. Creativity had solved our hat problem. And creativity was going to get me through Ms Adolf's essay. And not just get me through, either. My creativity was going to get me the best mark of my life.

Let everyone else write their stupid five paragraphs. Not me. Right then and there, I decided I was going to *build* my essay. I'd *bring* Niagara Falls into the classroom, water and all.

I could see it in my mind, just like I had seen the big hat for Cheerio. I'd build a living model of Niagara Falls, with cliffs and waterfalls and even a

boat. Everyone would know first hand what I had done in my summer holidays. Mr Love would hear about how great it was and come to our classroom just to see it. He'd call my dad and say what a great job I had done.

Papa Pete always says, "There are many roads to Rome." I used to think he was talking about the traffic in Italy. But now it made sense to me. What he meant was, if you can't get there one way, take another way. Like if you can't pull a rabbit out of a hat, pull a dachsund out. And if you can't write about Niagara Falls, *build* it.

My brain was on fire, and it felt good.

CHAPTER 9

Do you know what lucky is? Lucky is having friends who understand that building a magic hat can wait when Niagara Falls needs to be built right away. Lucky is having friends who don't make you feel stupid even though that's how you think of yourself. Lucky is having friends who don't make fun of you because some things – well, a lot of things – are hard.

I am so lucky.

As soon as I told Frankie and Ashley my idea about building Niagara Falls instead of writing the essay, they both volunteered to help.

"This is a big project," I said.

"We'd better make a list of supplies we'll need," Ashley suggested. "Frankie, you get a pencil and write the list."

"No way," he said. "I'm not a secretary. I'm a builder. A hammer-and-nails kind of guy."

"When was the last time you built anything?" Ashley asked him.

"Kindergarten," said Frankie. "Remember that awesome gingerbread house I made out of milk cartons and crackers?"

"I remember that it collapsed and then you ate it," I said.

"OK, you win. Hand me the pencil," Frankie said.

"The first thing we're going to need is water," I said. "Lots and lots of water."

"Newspaper and flour to build the cliffs," added Ashley.

"Twigs to make trees out of," I said.

"And rhinestones for the stars in the sky," said Ashley.

Frankie stopped writing.

"This isn't a T-shirt, Ashweena. Bear in mind, we are building one of the natural wonders of the world. Rhinestones have no place here."

"Then how about rocks for the cliffs," suggested Ashley.

"Rocks are good," said Frankie. He added "Rocks" to the list.

"Let's put a boat at the bottom of the falls," I said. "I must have a toy boat somewhere. And maybe I can get a spare pump from one of Emily's old fish tanks."

"What do you need a pump for?" asked Frankie.

"Something's got to push the water over the falls," I said.

"We better have a saucepan to collect the water," said Ashley. "A big saucepan."

I asked everyone to gather as much stuff as they could and meet the next night to begin building. We were all pretty excited – until we turned to leave, that is. Then we saw the worst thing you could possibly find in the doorway. Robert.

"Hi guys," he said with a grin. "Good news. My mum says I can join the meeting."

I've got to remember to tell his mother he's not invited.

"What are you guys doing?" he asked.

"Fourth-grade stuff," answered Frankie. "You wouldn't understand."

"Try me."

"We're building Niagara Falls," I said.

"More than six hundred thousand gallons of water flow over Niagara Falls every second," Robert said.

"How do you know that?" Ashley asked.

"Actually, it's all up here," Robert said, pointing to his head.

"Clear your throat, Robert," said Frankie.

Robert often gets this really annoying bubble in his throat when he talks, like he's got a little ball of spit down there. He'll just keep on talking if you don't tell him to clear that thing out.

"I bet you won't be able to create the mist," Robert went on. "Did you know that Niagara Falls produces enough mist to fill half the Grand Canyon every twenty minutes?"

Ashley thought for a minute. "As much as I hate to admit it, the mist does sound important," she whispered to me.

This gave Robert all the encouragement he

needed. "My mum has a fan she puts in the window on really hot days. We could use it to blow the water around to look like mist. I think she'd let us borrow it."

Oh great. Now it was *us*.

The next morning, I waited until Emily was in the shower and then went into her room. In her wardrobe, I found an old pump left over from when she had her Japanese fighting fish. I put the pump in a paper bag, along with a Lego boat from my toy chest. Then I went into the kitchen to find a saucepan. As I was clanking around in the cupboard, my mum came in.

"Hi honey. What are you looking for?"

"That big roasting tin you cook turkey in at Thanksgiving."

"Oh, I lent it to Mrs Fink. She was making a turkey for her son-in-law's birthday. Come to think of it, she never returned it."

"If it's OK with you, I'm going to get it back from her. I need it for a school project."

"Be sure to ask her how the turkey turned out," my mum said, as she put water on for tea. "I suggested she stuff it with wheatgrass and bean sprouts. I'm sure it was delicious."

I went next door to Flat 10B and knocked on the door. Mrs Fink answered. She isn't a small woman, and in her pink dressing gown, she looked like one of those giant pink elephants in the cartoons.

"Hankie!" she said. "Come in for a doughnut. I'll put my teeth in."

"That's OK, Mrs Fink," I said. "I have to get to school. I was just wondering if I could get our turkey tin back."

"Of course, darling," she said. She went to the kitchen and came back with the tin. As she handed it to me, Mrs Fink smiled and I thought I saw her gums. I took the tin and ran, without asking about the turkey.

After school, I took all my stuff to our clubhouse. Frankie had brought a big stack of newspapers. Ashley had a box of rocks and pebbles she had collected at Riverside Park. Even good old Robert showed up with a fan.

There's a sink in the broom cupboard down the hall, and I half filled the turkey tin with water. We let Robert do most of the newspaper shredding.

Ashley and I soaked the paper and mixed it with flour to make papier-mâché. As we built the cliffs, Ashley reminded me that we had to make a hole for the hose that was going to bring the water to the top of the falls.

The next day, we made another batch of papier-mâché and added it to the cliffs. A couple of times, the cliffs got so high that the papier-mâché slid down to the bottom. I had to prop it up while Ashley held her hair dryer up to it. Even then, it took two whole days and nights for the cliffs to dry.

Finally, the cliffs were ready for us to decorate. We put rocks and pebbles around to make them look real. Frankie had snipped some branches off the ficus tree in his living room when his mother wasn't looking. We stuck those along the top of the cliffs to look like trees.

On Saturday night, I decided it was time to add the water part. I had been collecting cardboard tubes from our flat. Three had come from rolls of paper towels and a couple of others from bathroom tissue. I love saying "bathroom tissue". It rolls off your tongue. Not like "toilet paper", which sounds too much like what it actually is.

If I do say so myself, I had come up with a great plan to get the water to the falls. I was going to connect the tubes with waterproof tape. Then I'd wrap the outside of this cardboard snake with clingfilm. We'd hook one end up to the hole we'd made in the cliffs and the other end up to the tap in the sink in our classroom. Connect the pump, turn on the water and hey presto, Niagara Falls.

"What are you doing?" asked Frankie, when he saw me wrapping the cardboard tubes in clingfilm.

I told him my brilliant plan.

"I don't know, Zip," he said, shaking his head. "Do you think that tube is going to be strong enough to hold water?

"Hey, if you can cover a bowl of watermelon with clingfilm and turn it upside down, then this will hold too," I assured him. "I tell you, water is going to sail through this baby."

On Sunday night, we had one final meeting to finish the project. I glued more trees on to the cliffs and put little Lego people into the boat. Ashley and I carefully attached the hose. We painted the cliffs brown – or, as Robert pointed out, burnt sienna. He's a real pain about vocabulary, that guy, but I have to admit, he was very helpful.

When Niagara Falls was finished, we all stood back to admire it.

"Don't move," Frankie said. "I'll be right back."

He disappeared. Two minutes later he was back, panting. He had run up six flights of stairs to his flat. When he's on a mission, Frankie never waits for the lift. He reached into his pocket and pulled out a gleaming baby-blue stone that I recognized right away. It was his best piece of turquoise from his private rock and mineral collection. Frankie put a spot of glue on it and placed the turquoise on top of the cliff.

"It's got good karma," he said.

He gave me his classic Big Dimple smile, then put out his hand. We did our secret handshake.

"You're going to knock 'em dead, Zip."

Didn't I tell you I was lucky?

That night, it was hard to sleep because I was so excited. I couldn't wait until morning when I'd take Niagara Falls to school and show everyone my living essay.

I heard the door creak open. My mum stuck her head in.

"All set for school tomorrow?" she asked.

"Yup."

"Are you sure you've finished your essay?" she whispered.

"It couldn't be any more complete, Mum."

"Do you need me to proofread it?"

"I'm telling you, Mum, it's perfect."

"I love you," she said.

"Me too," I said.

And she closed the door.

I stared up at the ceiling. All I could think about were the incredible things that were going to happen to me after I showed Niagara Falls. I made a list in my head.

TEN INCREDIBLE THINGS THAT WILL HAPPEN AFTER EVERYONE SEES MY NIAGARA FALLS PROJECT

BY HANK ZIPZER

1. I won't get just an A on it, I'll get the highest A they've ever given in America.
2. Ms Adolf will finally smile. (I wonder if her face will crack.)
3. They'll call an assembly for everyone in the school to see my project. Newspaper reporters will come. Television stations will bring their cameras.
4. I'll interview Frankie and Ashley on television. Maybe even Robert. Hmmm ... no, not Robert.
5. The mayor of Niagara Falls will come to shake my hand.
6. Head Teacher Love will declare a school holiday in my honour.

7. I'll be called to the White House to show my project to the president.
8. The president will be so impressed, he'll pass a law that kids in the fourth grade no longer have to write essays.
9. Every fourth-grade student in the country will break their number-two pencils in half.
10. Just before they do, they will all write me letters to say thank you. I'll have to get a secretary just to answer my fanmail.
11. I will never have to clear the table again. Emily, on the other hand, will have to do it until she's fifty-six.

I fell asleep with a smile on my face.

CHAPTER 11

OK, about the list in the last chapter. You're right. There are eleven things on it and I said there were only going to be ten. Well, you shouldn't be surprised. It's me, Hank Zipzer. I'm lucky that all my fingers and toes are attached. Otherwise, I'd lose count.

CHAPTER 12

When my alarm clock rang the next morning, I didn't hear the buzzer. All I heard was, "Monday morning, Monday morning, Monday morning." It was going to be tricky getting Niagara Falls to school, so we had to leave extra early. Ashley said her mum had to be at the hospital anyway, so she didn't mind walking us to school.

We met in the basement. Frankie and I each picked up one end of the tin. Since it was my project, I volunteered to be the one who walked backwards. Ashley held the water pump, the clingfilm-wrapped hose and a plastic bag with my costume in it. (I haven't mentioned the costume before, because

I threw it in at the last minute. I thought it would add what Papa Pete calls "pizazz".)

When we got outside our building, Ashley cleared the people out of the way and kept watch for big cracks in the pavement so I wouldn't trip. First we passed Mr Kim's market. He was putting out buckets of fresh flowers for the day. When he saw Niagara Falls, he took a flower from one of the buckets and put it on the top of the cliffs.

"Flowers grow on mountain top," he said.

"Thanks, Mr Kim," I said.

We reached the corner and waited for the lights to change. When they were red, we crossed Amsterdam Avenue. A couple of taxi drivers blew their horns as we walked by, probably because they were so amazed to see Niagara Falls passing by right in front of them. I felt good because a lot of them had probably never been to Niagara Falls, and at least now they were getting a chance to see it.

"Please! Hold your honks!" I shouted, as I took a half bow. "And thank you, one and all."

Frankie started to laugh, and then I did too. Ashley knew we were heading into one of our marathon laughing fits. When we were little, she watched us get plenty of time-outs at school because of our uncontrollable laughter.

"Stop it, boys!" she said. "Concentrate. You don't want to drop it now."

"Children, don't dawdle at the junction," Ashley's mum said. She had a good point. You can't fool around at a New York junction. When the lights change, the cars go. If you're in the way, it's your problem.

Dr Wong is very nice but very quiet. Ashley says she doesn't talk much because most of the people she is around all day are asleep. She's a surgeon.

We made it to the school zebra crossing without falling, tripping or dropping the project. We only had a few more steps to go, but they were tricky ones. There are a couple of big potholes in front of our school. They're always fixing them, but then other ones pop up. I heard once that potholes happen in the winter when there is ice and snow. Or maybe it's the traffic. No, I think it's the weather. When Emily was in kindergarten, I told her they were dragon footprints. Of course, it didn't scare her because, as we all know, she likes reptiles.

Our school is three storeys high. On the street side of the building, the bricks are covered with a big mural that was painted by some local New York artists. It shows a lot of kids with books open, sitting and reading happily under a rainbow. They sure didn't use me as a model.

When the road was clear, Mr Baker, the lollipop man, took us across.

"That's a mighty fine looking mountain you got there," he said to us.

"It's Niagara Falls, sir," I said.

"Well, it's a mighty fine looking Niagara Falls."

That made me feel good. Even though Mr Baker says nice things to all the kids, I like to think he really did like our project.

Finally, we reached the main door of PS 87. There were kids swarming all around the school, and we had to be careful not to get crunched. We were attracting a lot of attention.

"Keep your distance," I said to a bunch of first-graders who were hovering around us. "Important fourth-grade business coming through."

Ashley held the door open for us and we backed

into the corridor. We started the long climb to the second floor and our classroom. As luck would have it, the first person we saw when we got to the top was Nick McKelty.

"What is *that* supposed to be?" he asked in his usual creepoid manner.

I wasn't going to let this guy get to me.

"You just might be the only person in New York not to get it," I said. "We totally stopped traffic on Amsterdam Avenue. The taxis honked like we were a float in the Thanksgiving Day parade."

"Oh yeah?" McKelty said. "I was asked to ride on a float this year."

"Right, and my name is Bernice," Frankie said.

"In fact," McKelty went on, "they wanted me to be Santa Claus in the parade, but I said, 'Sorry, I'm already booked. Maybe next year.'"

"Breathe," Frankie said to himself. Then he turned to McKelty. "That's good," he said, "because your face would've scared all those little kids. It's such a drag seeing kids cry at a parade."

"Oh yeah?" McKelty answered.

"What a comeback," said Ashley. "You're quick, McKelty."

From around the corner, we heard the *squeak, squeak, squeak* of rubber on lino. That could only be Head Teacher Love. He always wears these black rubber-soled shoes that do up with two Velcro straps. I guess he has never learned to tie his laces.

"What have we here?" he boomed in his tall-man-bushy-hair voice.

We put Niagara Falls down on the floor.

"My summer holiday," I answered.

Nick stepped right in front of me.

"Our assignment is to do a five-paragraph essay on what we did this summer," said Nick. He gave Mr Love a smile that any sane person would describe as very, very icky. "*My* adventure was so exciting that *my* essay turned out to be *eight* paragraphs. And that's cutting it down from ten."

"Mr McKelty, you've got a future." Mr Love grinned. Then he turned to me. "And as for you, Mr Zipzer, don't be late for class."

He squeaked off down the hall. McKelty ran after him, continuing to blab in his ear – probably telling him how much he happens to love Velcro straps on shoes.

"Don't be late," I muttered under my breath. "Where does he think I'm going? To the dining room for a big breakfast?"

"Forget him," said Ashley. "You've got to keep your mind on what you're doing here."

I could still see McKelty walking down the hallway, talking to Mr Love like he was his best friend. Then I saw something truly disgusting.

"I don't believe it," I said. "McKelty's putting his arm round him!"

The McKelty Factor strikes again.

The bell rang and Nick came lumbering down the corridor towards us. Just before he turned into the classroom, he stopped and looked at me.

"I have a wonderful surprise in store for you, Zippity Zipzer," he said.

He gave me an annoying flick under the chin and slithered into class like the slimy snake he is.

CHAPTER 13

Ms Adolf was on the prowl. She was hungry for paper. "Please take your essays out, class," she said. "I hope you remembered to staple them in the upper-left-hand corner."

She walked up and down the aisles, clutching her register close to her chest. When she stopped at my desk, I could feel her hot breath on my head.

"Your desk appears to be empty, Mr Zipzer," she said.

My heart was pounding. This was the moment.

"I thought we agreed you were to read your essay first," she snapped.

"And I am completely, totally prepared, Ms Adolf," I said.

I looked at Frankie. I gave him a nod. He gave Ashley a nod. The three of us stood and went to our planned positions.

Ashley took the clingfilm-wrapped tube and attached it with tape to the tap at the sink. Frankie and I disappeared into the corridor.

"Excuse me!" Ms Adolf shouted. I think she was starting to get angry.

I stuck my head back into the classroom and said, "Get ready for creativity like you've never seen before."

Out in the corridor, we got my costume out of the plastic bag. Frankie held the yellow raincoat for me to slip into and I pulled on the boots and the fisherman's hat. Then we picked up the project and walked it into the classroom, where we placed it by the sink.

"Exactly what do you think you're doing?" Ms Adolf demanded to know.

"What you're about to see, Ms Adolf, is what I did in my summer holidays. My living essay."

The kids moved closer so they could see. Ryan Shimozato even stood up on his chair. Katie Sperling and Kim Paulson were whispering to each other and giggling. I noticed that Nick McKelty kept looking at the door to the classroom, like he was expecting someone.

Before Ms Adolf could object again, I began.

"Niagara Falls was formed twelve thousand years ago, but when I visited this summer, it didn't look a day over eleven thousand. It did, however, look wet – really wet."

That was Ashley's cue. She turned on the tap at the sink. With a quick twist of the nozzle, the water started to run through our hose and into the hole at the top of the papier-mâché cliff. I was so excited I couldn't continue. The falls were actually doing what they were supposed to do ... falling! The water hitting the bottom of the turkey tin sounded like rain.

Ashley turned on the fish tank pump and it started to bubble, moving the water from the bottom of the turkey tin back up to the top of the falls. The boat at the bottom of the tin rose in the water. It was floating! Everything was working!

"Seven hundred and fifty thousand gallons of water flow over these falls every second," I said. Old Robert had finally come in handy.

"Do you see that boat?" I asked, pointing to the Lego people in it. "Picture my mother, my father, my sister and me – dressed as I am now, covered with mist."

At that moment, Frankie turned on the fan, and a little of the water started to blow towards my raincoat. The kids gasped.

"Awesome," said Ryan Shimozato.

"Truly awesome," said Justin, Ricky and Gerald. They're Ryan's crew and they like whatever he likes.

"Half the falls are in Canada, and the other half are in the United States, making Niagara Falls a link between our two countries," I went on. I remembered the tour guide had said that while we were waiting in line to get on the boat. I was on a roll. I knew so many facts about Niagara Falls, I could've gone on until lunch or longer.

Out of the corner of my eye, I saw that Frankie was trying to get my attention. I glanced over at him. He whispered something, but I couldn't quite understand him. It sounded like "no peeking". I didn't know what he was talking about. I shrugged and went on.

"We left New York City on a muggy August morning," I said, pretending to be driving in a car. "My mother said it was so hot you could fry eggs on her knees."

The kids laughed. They were loving this. I really felt wonderful and successful. *Maybe I'll be a stand-up comedian when I grow up,*

I thought. *Take this show on the road.* I looked at Frankie. He wasn't laughing. Why not?

Whatever he had been trying to say to me, he said again. "No peeking"? Was that it? I still couldn't understand him. He sure was flapping his arms around a lot.

Just then, the door swung open. In walked Leland Love. Wow, this was great. The head teacher *was* coming to see my project, just like I had hoped.

"Tourists from all over the world come to see Niagara Falls," I said. I was getting more and more confident by the minute. "A couple from Italy asked me to take their picture with the falls in the background," I added. I hadn't even planned to tell that part of the story. It just came out.

Suddenly, Frankie walked in front of me and with an Italian accent said, "I thinka thesa falls are betta than SpaghettiOs."

The class howled.

"SpaghettiOs rule!" Luke Whitman laughed. "SpaghettiOs forget-ios!" It doesn't take much for Luke to go out of control.

"What are you doing?" I whispered to Frankie. "You weren't supposed to talk."

"I've been trying to tell you," Frankie whispered. "We're leaking! Look!"

I looked over at the hose. Oh no, this wasn't happening. The cardboard was soaking wet. The tube was turning to mush and the last piece of tape holding the hose to the cliffs was coming loose. I yelled for Ashley to turn off the water. She ran to the sink, but she was so nervous, she turned the water on full force instead, which totally blew the hose off the project. Water sprayed everywhere, but mostly on Ms Adolf. She opened her mouth to speak and got a mouthful of falls.

The hose started to spin around, and the kids all ran for cover, laughing and shouting. Ms Adolf was so stunned, she just stood there. *Bam!* She got pelted again with a blast of water. When she put her hands up to her face to block the water, her register fell to the floor. It landed in a puddle of water. She gasped and tried to reach for it, but Luke Whitman was running wild and stamped on it, pushing it completely underwater.

Ms Adolf stared at her register. The paper was absorbing water fast and turning into a soggy mess.

She opened her mouth wide, like she was going to scream really loudly, but all that came out was a mouse-like "eeeeekkk".

Bam! The hose came around again and hit her with another shot of water. She was really

wet now. It looked like she had just stepped out of the shower with her clothes on. The pile of grey hair that was always neatly pinned on top of her head fell down and looked like a horse's tail.

"The water!" Mr Love yelled. "Someone turn

off the water!" The kids were all laughing pretty hard, so no one moved towards the sink. Mr Love bolted across the room. He had to push past Luke Whitman, who was leading a bunch of kids in a rain dance. There was so much water on the floor, the classroom looked like a pond. Pencils, crayons, Ms Adolf's register and even a tuna fish sandwich in a bag floated by.

Mr Love sloshed over to the sink. As he reached the counter, he stepped on the bag. It exploded and the tuna sandwich squished out from under his shoe. It was a slippery mess. Mr Love went sliding on the sandwich like he was on water skis. The last thing I saw before he went swimming was his hand reaching for the counter with the turkey tin on it. As the tin tipped, the papier-mâché flew and the muddy, mushy Niagara Falls landed with a splat all over Mr Love's face.

I didn't mean to laugh, but I couldn't stop. In fact, I was laughing so hard that I fell bum-first into the water. Then what do I see but Nick McKelty's hand reaching out to Mr Love.

"Don't worry, sir," he said. "I'll save you."

Sometimes I think things happen the way they're

supposed to, because Nick McKelty, suck-up of the century, slipped too and went flying headfirst into the muck. When he came up for air, he looked like he had a papier-mâché chicken sitting on his head. He wiped his face and leaned over to Head Teacher Love.

"Didn't I tell you Zipzer was about to launch a disaster?" he said.

Oh, so *that's* why Head Teacher Love had come to class. McKelty, that rat, had told him to come and see me make a fool of myself. And stupid me thought it was because he had heard I had a great project.

Head Teacher Love didn't say a word. All he did was wag a finger at me. I knew what that meant.

"I'll see you in my office … now!"

CHAPTER 14

The corridor is a lonely place when you're sitting on the bench outside the head teacher's office. Kids you know walk by on the way to the toilets or the water fountain, but no one says hello to you. No one even looks at you. It's like you're wearing a sign round your neck that says TROUBLE – KEEP AWAY.

I had been waiting in the corridor for more than an hour. They were inside – the three of them, Mr Love and the Zipzers. That would be Stan and Randi. Also known as Mum and Dad.

It was hard to sit still. I got up and asked Mrs Crock in the attendance office if I could have a pencil and paper, just to doodle or something.

"You're supposed to be using this time to think about what you've done," she said.

"I think better when I doodle," I told her.

"So do I," she said. She gave me a piece of paper and her pencil. That was nice of her.

When I went back into the corridor, Mr Love was standing outside his office. He didn't speak – he just wagged his finger, inviting me in. It's the kind of invitation you don't say no to.

As I entered the office, I could tell my father was really angry. I knew that because his bum was hovering above the chair cushion, not quite touching it.

"Can I say something?" I said.

"Absolutely not," answered Mr Love. "I think your actions have spoken loudly enough."

I noticed that Mr Love's office smelled a little like tuna. *It must be from his shoes,* I thought. He had changed his shirt, but he still had some papier-mâché stuck to his cheek. It was right above his Statue of Liberty mole. I couldn't help thinking that the Statue of Liberty finally had a torch.

"What you did today in class was completely irresponsible," Mr Love said.

I turned to my father. He would understand. "But, Dad, what I was trying to do—"

My father stood up. "Are you aware of the chaos you have created, Hank? First of all, you didn't follow the rules. You can't just make up your own assignment."

"Yes, but I wanted to—"

"Don't interrupt your father," my mother said. I couldn't believe it. Even Mum was on their side. I thought maybe it was the shoes. She usually wears sandals, but she had put on her black leather loafers, the ones that look like Ms Adolf's shoes. She's not as much fun when she wears those shoes.

"You were supposed to write an essay. Five paragraphs. That's with a pencil, Hank. Not papier-mâché." My father was seriously mad.

"But, Dad, I remembered every fact I learned on our trip. I was writing it with my mouth. Like, did you know that Niagara Falls is two thousand two hundred and twenty feet wide, and it's one hundred and seventy-three feet high, and—"

"Enough of this," interrupted Mr Love. "We are here to decide on an appropriate punishment for what you've done."

At this moment I realized that the president of the United States was not going to be inviting me to the White House.

"Detention for two weeks," Head Teacher Love said.

"Grounded at home," my father added. "Same length of time."

My brain froze. Two weeks! The magic show – oh no! The magic show was right in the middle of my punishment.

I'm dead. I'm doomed. I'm out of the Magik 3.

CHAPTER 15

I left Head Teacher Love's office and headed downstairs to the dining room. A couple of first-graders passed me on their way to the library.

"I think that's the boy who got into trouble," one of them whispered loudly. They stared at me like I had just robbed a bank or something. I spilled a little water on the floor. Big deal. OK, a lot of water. OK, a *whole* lot of water.

What does a guy do in this situation? I figured the only thing to do was wave. I went into my best Hank Zipzer strut.

"Good to see you," I said, grinning at them. "What's up in show-and-tell today?"

I think I scared them because they ran away. I continued downstairs. Some kids were already leaving the dining room and heading out to the playground. I passed Ryan and Gerald. Ryan held up his hand for a high five.

"You're a riot, man," he said.

"Truly," said Justin and Ricky, who were following behind.

"Your buddies are still eating lunch at your usual spot," Ryan said, pointing in the general direction of our table.

I went over to the table and slid in next to Ashley. She was in the middle of telling Frankie and Robert how she was going to spend her money from the magic show.

"I already have nine dollars saved," she was saying. "With the ten dollars we'll each earn, I'll have enough to get the dolphin which will complete my crystal sea family."

"I'd hold off on that dolphin," I said.

"How bad was Mr Love?" Frankie asked. "Paint the picture, Zip."

"It was ugly," I answered. "I didn't get one word in. What I did get was two weeks of detention at school and two weeks of being grounded at home."

"With or without TV?" asked Frankie.

"That is without any electronic device known to mankind," I said.

Frankie grabbed his heart and fell to the ground. "Just the thought of it makes me stop breathing."

"Of course they're going to let you out for the magic show," Ashley said. She was twirling her ponytail in her fingers, which she does when she's worried.

"No," I answered. I didn't have the courage to look at her. "They said no exceptions."

"I can take his place," Robert chimed in.

"No, you can't," we answered together.

As if what was happening wasn't bad enough, suddenly a dark cloud appeared. Its name was Nick McKelty.

"Oh, poor thing, did Head Teacher Love bust you hard?" the big creep said in this stupid baby voice. His teeth were looking especially wonky.

"Hank got two weeks' detention," Robert volunteered. As you've probably already noticed, Robert doesn't know when to keep his mouth shut.

"What are you going to do about your grandpa's magic show at my dad's bowling alley?" Nick said. "Sounds like it's not happening." He was really enjoying this.

Before I had a chance to answer, he threw his big, slimy arm round me. He put his face up to mine, and there it was – the bad breath again. I didn't breathe.

"Hey, don't worry about it, Zipper man," he said. "I got you covered."

"*You?*" I said, taking a breath and removing his arm from my shoulder. "What can *you* do, McKelty?"

"I'll put on a bowling show. I'll knock down more pins than ... than ... than..." I could see him searching for something clever to say, but as usual, he came up empty.

"I'll knock down a whole lot of pins," he finally spat out. "I just have to decide if I should use my left hand or my right hand."

"For your information," said Ashley, "the bowling league doesn't want to see *bowling*. They know how to do that. They want to see *magic*. That's why they hired us."

"My ball handling *is* magical," McKelty said. He was really happy with that comeback. He reached over and in one swipe his apelike hand nabbed Robert's Jelly swirl and Ashley's Nestlé Crunch right off the table.

"Don't feel bad," he said as he walked away. "There's always next year."

We were silent. We didn't feel bad. We felt horrible.

"Hey, come on, guys," I said with fake cheerfulness. "You can do the show without me!"

"We can't build the hat without you," said Ashley. "You're the one who knows how to do everything."

"Besides, who do you think is going to get Cheerio inside the hat?" asked Frankie. "Do you think that dog is going to listen to me? Not in this century."

I knew they were right. I had ruined everything for them.

I told them I was sorry.

But I don't think it helped.

CHAPTER 16

The bell rang at three o'clock. Everyone grabbed their rucksacks and headed for the door. They were on their way to football practice or sax lessons or other fun after-school activities. But not me. Nope. I was about to start my first day of detention. It was going to be me in a chair and Ms Adolf at her desk for the next fun-filled hour.

I must have really sighed loudly.

"Do you have something to say?" Ms Adolf asked.

I didn't say a word. I made a sound. The human body does that sometimes.

"Henry," Ms Adolf said, "I assume you want to use this time wisely."

"Yes, Ms Adolf," I answered. I couldn't imagine Ms Adolf having a first name. Maybe her friends just call her Ms Adolf.

"I've decided to have you write your essay under my supervision," she said. "Using paper and pencil, Henry. No monkey business this time."

I don't know why people always think monkey business is a bad thing. I love monkeys. They always seem to have such a good time, picking bugs off one another and eating them.

I took out a piece of paper and stared at it. It was blank. *So* blank. Ms Adolf sat down at her desk and began to write in her brand-new register. Neither one of us made a sound. It was so quiet, I could hear her breathing.

The clock on the wall clicked and the big hand jerked forward. One minute down, fifty-nine to go. Suddenly, the classroom door flew open and a messenger from the office came in. She handed Ms Adolf a note and disappeared just as quickly. After Ms Adolf had read the note, she got her handbag out of the bottom drawer.

"I have an emergency that I have to deal with," she said. Her pet fire-breathing dragon must be sick.

"My husband's car won't start and I have to pick him up from work."

Husband? Someone married her? No way. Do you think he kisses her goodnight?

I must have wrinkled up my face, because Ms Adolf said, "What's the face for, Henry?"

"Umm ... I was just thinking about ... umm ... how it would feel for a raisin to try to lift up an elephant," I said.

"You would do better to keep your mind on your work, Henry, and not fill your head with silly thoughts." Ms Adolf put the register in the top drawer and locked it with her shiny key. She scribbled a note on a Post-it and gave it to me.

"The office has arranged for you to spend the rest of the hour in the music room with Mr Rock, the music teacher. He's on his way. Go there and give him this note. Sit quietly until he arrives."

The music room is in the basement. Even though it's right next to the dining room, I don't go there unless I have to. Being there makes me remember my second-grade choir audition, which I've been trying to forget ever since it happened. That was when Mrs Peacock, the music teacher, told me that if I wanted to be in the choir, I couldn't sing out loud. I was only allowed to mouth the words so I wouldn't throw everyone else off key. Mrs Peacock left last year to have a baby. I had never met Mr Rock. He was new.

The first things I noticed when I went into the music room were the posters all around the walls. Most of them were of composers – Beethoven and Mozart and all those old guys. But there were other posters too – cool ones. Pink Floyd. A super-sized photo of Manhattan from the air. An action shot of Michael Jordan going up for a tomahawk dunk. And my favourite, a picture of the coolest 1959 red-and-white Corvette you've ever seen.

A whole bunch of instruments were spread out in the room. There were triangles and xylophones and a piano. I sat down in a chair facing a set of silver-and-burgundy drums. I realized that my leg was bouncing up and down, about a mile a minute. It does that sometimes when I'm supposed to be sitting still.

As I sat there, it hit me that I had two whole weeks of misery in front of me. It didn't seem fair.

I was being punished for trying to do my best.

Thoughts started coming from every corner of my brain. I wished Mr Love had let me finish just one sentence. I wished my parents had given me a chance to tell them how much I know about Niagara Falls. I wished I was as smart as my sister. She could do anything. She has just toilet-trained her parakeet. My parents are always so proud of her.

I picked up one of the drumsticks and tapped the big drum. It felt good. I liked the sound. I hit it again, a little louder. Then I picked up the other stick and looked around to make sure I was still alone. *Bam!* I hit the drum, first with one stick, then the other. *Bam, bam, bam.* The drums were starting to sound like I felt.

Bam. I wish I didn't always forget my rucksack.

Bam. I wish I could do long division.

Bam. I wish I didn't feel so stupid all the time.

Before I knew it, I was hitting the drums so fast I could hardly see my hands. The cymbal was right in front of me. Why not? I hit it. *Clash.* The sound vibrated all around the room. I smacked it again. Now back to the drums. *Bam, clash, boom!*

"That's for detention!" I shouted.

Clash, boom, bam!

"That's for always getting into trouble!" My voice rang out.

Bam, bam, bammitty bam!

"That's five, one for each paragraph I can't write!"

Bam, boom, bam, boom, bam, boom, boom!

"And that's for my stupid brain!" I yelled.

From behind me, I heard a man's voice say, "I bet your brain isn't stupid."

I froze, then slowly turned round. The man in the doorway had a young face but a head full of curly, silver hair. He was wearing a blue denim shirt and a tie with musical notes on it.

"Mr Rock?" I asked.

"That's me," he answered. "Does your band have a CD out yet?"

"I'm really sorry," I said. "I know I wasn't supposed to touch these, but—"

"They're instruments," Mr Rock said. "They're here to play. Sounds like they helped you express yourself."

"I've had a bad day," I said.

"Because of your stupid brain?" he asked.

"Yeah. How did you know?"

"Because you just said it," he said with a smile. "It was hard to miss."

I handed Mr Rock the note from Ms Adolf.

He read it, then pulled up a chair and sat down backwards on it. I assumed he was going to ask me why I was in detention, but he didn't.

"So your name is Henry Zipzer?" he said.

"My friends call me Hank."

"Hank, that's a good name," he said. "Ever heard of Hank Aaron?"

"April the eighth, 1974," I answered. "The day Hammerin' Hank beat Babe Ruth's home-run record."

"I'm a baseball fan, too," he said. "I don't suppose you know what number home run Hank Aaron hit on that day."

"Seven hundred and fifteen. Do you want to know a weird Hank Aaron fact?"

"Sure," said Mr Rock.

"In four of his twenty-three seasons in baseball, Hank Aaron hit exactly forty-four home runs, which was his uniform number. Pretty amazing, huh?"

"Seems to me," said Mr Rock, "that your brain isn't as stupid as you think. It's got plenty of good information tucked inside it."

"I don't have a problem remembering interesting

facts," I explained. "I just can't do a lot with them. Like writing essays and spelling are tough – stuff that's easy for everyone else."

"Everybody learns differently," he said. "*Your* brain is *your* brain. You just have to figure out the right way to feed it."

"I gave it a lot of Cocoa Pops this morning," I said.

"How about music?" He laughed. "Do you ever feed it music?"

He actually waited for an answer.

"No," I said.

Mr Rock rubbed his hands together as though he was about to eat something delicious.

"I'll make a deal with you," he said. "Ms Adolf's note says you're supposed to work on your essay. We've got forty-five minutes of detention left. Let's take a few minutes to listen to some music. It might put you in the writing mood. What do you like?"

"Well, my essay is supposed to be about Niagara Falls."

"Let me see if I can find some water music," he said. "What does Niagara Falls sound like?"

"It sounded like thunder when I was there."

He shuffled through some CDs and picked one out.

"This is part of the Grand Canyon Suite," he said. "It's called *Cloud Burst*." He put it on, then turned it up loud. It really felt as though it was raining right there in the basement of PS 87. I'm not kidding.

Papa Pete says that you never know where good luck is going to come from. In my case, it came from Big Harry's Auto and Body Shop, which took the entire week to fix Mr Adolf's car. Ms Adolf had to leave early every day to pick up her husband, so I got to spend one whole week of detention with Mr Rock.

He taught me how to play "Hey Jude" on the xylophone. We looked at magazine pictures of our favourite cars. I picked the Ferrari F-50 convertible and he picked a 1947 Ford Woody with a surfboard on top. He put me in complete charge of trimming the dead leaves off his indoor plants. I liked that job.

We worked on my essay too. When I got stuck, which was every other second of every other minute, he'd ask me questions like "How did the falls make you feel?" or "What did you like best about the trip?" That really helped me focus.

The best part was listening to music. He'd put on a CD and then we'd just sit back and let music fill the room.

It felt so good, I couldn't believe I was at school.

CHAPTER 17

"What's a nine-letter French word for eggplant?" my father shouted to no one in particular.

I was sitting at the other end of the dining-room table, doodling in my maths workbook. As part of my punishment, my parents had taken away my privacy privileges. I wasn't allowed to do my homework in my bedroom. The worst part was having to listen to my father's crossword puzzle questions. I don't get it. What's the point of doing crossword puzzles if you have to ask everyone else for the answers?

Emily walked out of her bedroom with Katherine on her shoulder. Her long tongue was darting in and out of her mouth – Katherine's tongue, that is, not Emily's.

"Has anyone seen Katherine's bag of dinner pellets?" Emily asked.

"I put them in the cookie jar, honey," Mum called from the kitchen.

"Mum!" I yelled. "I ate those for my snack this afternoon. I thought they were one of your new healthy treats."

Emily laughed. Katherine jiggled up and down on her shoulder.

"It's not funny," I said. "Now I'll probably grow a long, disgusting iguana tongue."

As I was rinsing my mouth out at the kitchen sink, the doorbell rang.

"I'll get it!" I yelled.

"Remember to look through the spyhole first," Mum reminded me.

If I stand on my toes, I can just about get my eye up to the spyhole. I looked out but didn't see anyone.

"Who is it?" I shouted through the door.

"It's us," Frankie whispered. "Open up, Zip."

I pressed my face up against the crack in the door. "I'm grounded," I whispered back. "You know I can't play."

"We're not here to see you," Frankie said. "We're here to talk to your dad."

I opened the door. Frankie and Ashley marched right past me, with Robert bringing up the rear.

"Good evening, Mr Z.," Frankie said, going right up to my father.

"We've come to discuss a very important business matter," added Ashley.

My father looked up from his crossword puzzle.

"You kids aren't supposed to be here," he said.

"Hank is still grounded for another week."

"This matter can't wait," said Ashley.

"Aubergine," said Robert, looking at the newspaper in my father's hand.

"What's that supposed to mean?" snapped Frankie.

"It means eggplant in French," said Robert, pointing at the blank spaces on my father's crossword puzzle. "Thirteen across is *aubergine*."

"Sometimes you scare me," Frankie said to Robert.

"Come on, boys, let's not forget why we're here," Ashley said. She turned to my father, with her no-nonsense face on. "Mr Zipzer, as you know, Magik 3 has a contract with Papa Pete to put on a fantastic magic show this weekend at McKelty's Roll 'N Bowl. We've tried all week to build the special hat we need for the grand finale. But our hat looks like a sofa."

"We're begging you, Mr Z.," said Frankie. "We're *pleading* with you. Free Hank. We can't make the hat without him."

My father shook his head no.

"I'll help you with forty-three down," Robert offered. "Oh, I also happen to know three across."

"I'm afraid Hank has to learn his lesson," my father interrupted. "There'll be other magic shows."

He stood up, went to the front door and held it open. You couldn't get a much more final "no" than that. Frankie, Ashley and Robert left. My father closed the door and started back to his chair. The doorbell rang again. My father span round and yanked the door open.

"Now listen, kids," he began. Then he stopped suddenly. The next thing I heard was him saying, "I'm sorry, can I help you?"

I got up to see who was at the front door.

What is Mr Rock doing here? Oh no. I bet I broke the drum and he's here to tell my parents. I hit myself on the forehead with my fist. Not hard, but like I do sometimes when I'm frustrated with myself. How could I have been so stupid?

"I hope I'm not interrupting your dinner," Mr Rock said. "I'm Donald Rock, the music teacher from PS 87. I was wondering if I could talk to you for a moment?"

My father opened the door wider and led Mr Rock into the living room.

I was surprised to see him. I had never had a teacher pop by before. But then again, Mr Rock wasn't like other teachers.

"What's he doing here?" Emily whispered to me. "You must have messed up big-time."

My mother came out of the kitchen, drying her hands on a green checked tea towel. She picked up a plate from the dining-room table and offered Mr Rock a cracker with some of her new soy cheddar cheese spread. He popped it into his mouth before I had a chance to warn him. His lips stuck together when he tried to talk.

"I had the pleasure of spending last week with your son during his detention," Mr Rock began. He scraped some of the soy cheese off the roof of his mouth, trying to smile at the same time. My mother offered him another cracker but, smart guy that he is, Mr Rock said no thanks.

"I've had a lot of time to talk to Hank and to observe him. I've noticed that he is somewhat frustrated about his schoolwork," he said.

"Very frustrated," my mother added.

"Mr and Mrs Zipzer, I believe Hank might benefit from being tested – to see if he has any learning difficulties." Mr Rock waited for their answer.

"There's nothing wrong with Hank," my father said. "If he spent as much time doing his schoolwork as he does daydreaming and mooching around his room and building things, he'd be an *A* student. Hank is just lazy."

"Maybe that's not the case," Mr Rock said.

"You know, many children have learning difficulties. Every child's brain is wired differently."

Every brain is wired differently? What was he saying? That my brain is messed up? Oh that's great. Now everyone really will think I'm stupid!

"What does that mean, 'wired differently'?" my mum asked.

"Different kids learn in different ways," Mr Rock said. "I know that because I myself had difficulty at school."

"Hank's sister, Emily, is an excellent student," my father said. "She doesn't seem to have any problems at school."

Emily held an iguana pellet in the palm of her hand. Katherine whipped out her long tongue and snapped it up. I'll tell you one thing – Emily may not have school problems, but she has weird taste in pets.

"I'm sure you're very proud of Emily," Mr Rock continued, "but having a sister who excels adds to the pressure on Hank."

"What pressure?" said my father. "Hank doesn't worry about anything. *That's* his problem."

My mother was studying me very carefully.

My leg was bouncing up and down again. She was watching it.

"Stan, can we at least talk about this?" she asked.

"I think that's a good idea," Mr Rock said. "You have a lot to think about. I just thought it was better to have this conversation in person rather than on the phone. Give me a call if you want to talk further."

Mr Rock turned to me. "Hank, we've been talking *about* you but not *to* you. Do you have any questions?"

"Just one," I said. "Let's say a person in the fourth grade might have learning difficulties. And that person wanted to do something that was very creative, like for example a magic show, which included earning, let's say, a ten-dollar bill. Don't you think that person should be allowed to do it because he tries so hard at everything?"

"I think creativity should always be encouraged." Mr Rock smiled.

He stood up to go. He shook hands with everybody, including Katherine. She must have liked him too, because her tongue shot out and gave his hand a sticky lick.

As soon as Mr Rock had gone, I turned to my parents.

"You wouldn't go against the advice of a teacher, would you?" I asked. I had great hope in my heart. "Please … can I just do the magic show?"

My mother and father looked at each other for what seemed like a year and a half.

"We'll get back to you on this," my father finally answered.

CHAPTER 18

They got back to me the next morning.

They said yes.

The show was on!

Magik 3 was back in business. I was so excited that if you hold this book to your ear, you can hear me jumping up and down.

CHAPTER 19

At exactly seven o'clock on Saturday night, we pushed the giant hat through the swing doors of McKelty's Roll 'N Bowl. If I do say so myself, the hat was awesome. It was big and black and it had wheels. We had even built the secret pocket inside where Cheerio could hide until it was time to pull him out. To keep him happy, we put doggie treats inside the pocket with him.

McKelty's was jammed with people. It was opening night for the bowling league season. There were twelve teams. Each had their own lane and their own T-shirts. Papa Pete and The Chopped Livers were on lane five warming up. In the middle of the bowling alley, where they usually serve pizza at birthday parties, my mum had put out sandwiches. Papa Pete had warned her that anything with soy was out of the question. It had to be the real thing. I could smell the hot pastrami on fresh rye bread. My mouth started to water, but I knew we had more important things to do before we ate.

"Attention, bowlers," came a voice from the loudspeaker. I knew that voice.

"Magik 3 couldn't be with us tonight because one of its members was grounded for being too stupid to write his essay," the voice said.

The McKelty Factor strikes again.

"Instead we have something much better – a thrilling, unbelievable, death-defying bowling exhibition that stars me."

Trust Nick McKelty to put together a show starring only himself.

"That slimy toad thinks he's taking our spot," Ashley said.

"Yeah, well, I hope that slimy toad can swim because I'm going to flush him down the toilet," Frankie growled.

The loudspeaker crackled again. "For my first

feat, I'm going to bowl a strike with my left hand. Blindfolded."

Before we knew it, Nick appeared on lane ten. The jerk was actually wearing a blindfold. Everyone watched as he brought the ball up to his chest. On his bowling ball was a big picture of his slimy face. Unbelievable!

He took one, two, three steps towards the line and let the ball fly off his fingers. It landed on the lane with a *thud* and rolled smack into the gutter. The crowd groaned. I knew this was our opportunity.

I jumped up on to one of the benches and said, "Ladies and gentlemen, how about that Nick McKelty, the bowling whizz – doesn't he look great in a blindfold? Let's give it up for him."

Everyone laughed. I motioned for Frankie and Robert to wheel out the hat.

Nick looked stunned. He tried to take off his blindfold, but he had tied the knot too tightly.

"While we're setting up for the real entertainment, take a moment to enjoy the mouth acrobatics of Miss Ashley Wong, as she tries to tie not one but *two* cherry stems into a knot, never once using her hands," I said with pride.

I handed Ashley two cherries from the bar. She popped them into her mouth, scrunching up her face and moving her tongue a mile a minute. As she worked, she strolled around the audience, showing off her T-shirt with the red rhinestone cherries. By the time she got back to where she had begun, she had produced two knotted cherry stems, connected at the top. They looked like a small Christmas tree. Papa Pete led the applause.

Frankie gave me the nod. He was ready to go.

"Now, ladies and gentlemen, for the main event, I'm happy to present the freestyling magic of Frankie Townsend and Magik 3," I announced.

"Hey, what about my bowling tricks?" Nick McKelty shouted. He had finally managed to untie his blindfold. His eyes looked blazing mad. "I'm not finished yet."

"Yes, you are!" the crowd yelled back.

Nick ran into his father's office to sulk.

Frankie started right away on his act. He pulled scarves from his sleeve, cut a rope into three pieces and put it back together and pushed a pencil through the centre of a quarter that he borrowed from Papa Pete. That truly is one of my favourite tricks. And Frankie, that rat, won't tell me how he does it.

Ashley and Robert wheeled out the hat while I kept watch on Cheerio, trying to keep him calm. He was getting that look in his eye, his pre-spinning look.

"Not now, Cheerio," I whispered to him, reaching into the hat to scratch him between the ears. He loves that. "Don't go crazy on me, boy."

"And now, for my grand finale," announced Frankie. "At the special request of Papa Pete, I will pull a small live furry thing from this magical top hat!"

"It's probably a stuffed teddy bear," McKelty shouted from the office doorway. "I'm sure everyone would rather see me throw a strike backwards, between my legs, again using my left hand. Wouldn't you?"

It was his father who gave him the answer everyone else was thinking.

"Be quiet, Nick," he said, "and enjoy the show."

"Here we have a hat," Frankie began, pointing to our giant top hat. "My assistants will show you the inside of the hat." Ashley and I tipped the hat forward so everyone could see inside. Cheerio was tucked in his secret pocket so you couldn't see him. I thought I heard a tiny yip as he slid against the side.

"Notice that it's actually empty," Robert said with this kind of goofy smile. We had decided to give him a line.

"I will now take my cape and cover the hat," Frankie said. He showed the audience both sides of the cape and laid it over the hat like a tablecloth. The place was silent, except if you stood close enough to the hat, you could hear the *crunch, crunch, crunch* of doggie treats inside Cheerio's mouth.

"Hank, the magic words, if you please," Frankie said.

I stepped forward, closed my eyes and waved my hands over the cape. We hadn't rehearsed that part, but I thought it added a lot to the moment. I chanted:

"Something live, something furry,
Appear now, in a hurry!"

"Zengawii!" Frankie shouted as he pulled the cape off the hat. People in the audience moved to the edge of their seats. Everyone was completely quiet. Frankie reached into the hat. Suddenly there was a sound! It was the growl of one very angry little dog. Frankie pulled his hand out of the hat really fast. Cheerio stuck his face out, his paws hanging over the

brim of the hat. He looked at the audience. I don't
think he'd ever seen so many people in one place.

The audience burst into laughter and applause,
which must have really scared Cheerio, because he
dived back into the bottom of the hat and started
to spin. And I don't mean just normal spinning.
No, this was mega-spinning. He was going so fast
that the hat started to move down a lane.

"Is this part of the trick?" I whispered to Frankie.

"He's your dog, Zip. Don't ask me," he answered.

By that time, the hat was rocketing down the lane. It turned round and round, picking up speed

from the oil on the wood. In no time, it was at the end of the lane. *Smack!* The hat crashed into the pins, sending them flying in every direction. Nine pins went down. The last one teetered back and forth, back and forth. Almost ... yes ... no ... yes ... finally, it fell.

The crowd gasped.

"How about that for a strike!" Papa Pete yelled.

The place went wild. Everyone was applauding – everyone but Nick McKelty. He just stood by the sandwiches, scowling.

"Hey, doesn't anyone want to see my world-famous left-handed trick shot?" he yelled.

"Give it up, Nick!" I said to him. "You can't top the hat!"

He was so mad, his face turned bright red.

"Fine," he said. "Then I'm getting a Vanilla Coke. And you can't have one!"

"Is he the comeback king or what?" Ashley said. We all laughed as he stomped off.

Cheerio was out of the hat by now, sliding down the lane as he tried to make his way towards me. He looked like he was on ice skates. I think he was still feeling dizzy, because his eyes were spinning in opposite directions. I scooped him up and gave him a big hug.

I turned round. All the people in the bowling alley were on their feet cheering – for Cheerio and for us, the Magik 3.

Frankie, Ashley, Robert and I joined hands and took a bow. It was the greatest feeling of my entire life.

CHAPTER 20

There's a little balcony off our living room. It's my favourite place because at night you can see the moon from there. As I sat on the balcony and looked up at the moon, I thought about how great it feels to actually do something right.

Papa Pete slid the door open and brought out two pickles – my favourite bedtime snack. Mine was an old dill and his was a crunchy garlic. He sat down next to me and said, "You should be very proud of yourself tonight, Hank."

"I really am," I said.

We were quiet for a while, just sitting there, enjoying our pickles.

"They want to test me," I said finally.

"In what, maths?" Papa Pete asked.

"A teacher came over to our house. He said I might have learning difficulties. He said my brain might be different."

"We're all different," said Papa Pete. "That's what makes us great."

"But what if the test shows that I'm stupid?"

"Grandson of mine, there is nothing stupid about you. Didn't you build that project for school? Didn't you figure out how to make the hat work? Didn't you amaze every one of my friends tonight at the bowling alley? You're a winner, Hank."

"But I'm different."

"Take pickles," said Papa Pete. "There are big ones and little ones, smooth ones and bumpy ones, very crunchy ones and not-so-crunchy ones. There are bread-and-butter pickles, gherkins, hamburger slices, half-dills, full-dills…"

"OK, Papa Pete, I get the picture."

"The point is this," he said. "They're all different and they're all delicious to someone. And you, my grandson, are positively delicious."

I looked down at the little bit of pickle I had left. I popped it into my mouth. It was really good.

Then I looked at Papa Pete. He really knows a lot about everything. I sure hope he's right about me!

An interview with Henry Winkler

What's your favourite thing about Hank Zipzer?

My favourite thing about Hank Zipzer is that he is resourceful. Just because he can't figure something out doesn't mean that he won't find a way. I love his sense of humour. Even though Lin and I write the books together, when we meet in the morning to work we never know where the characters or the story will take us. Hank and his friends make us laugh all the time.

Hank likes to write lists. Are you a list person, too? (If so, what sorts of lists do you make?)

Hank likes to write lists, and so do I. My whole life is organized on scraps of paper in a pile on my desk by my phone. If I didn't make lists, I would get nothing done, because I would forget the important things that I had to do. And then, I'm constantly rewriting those lists and adding to them. So yes, I'm a list maker.

Who was your favourite teacher?

Believe it or not, Mr Rock, the music teacher at my high school, McBurney's School for Boys, was my favourite teacher. He seemed to understand that learning was difficult for me. He understood that just because I had trouble with almost every subject, it did not mean I was stupid.

Where did you grow up?

I grew up on the West side of New York City in the same building Hank lives in. The neighbourhood, the stores, the park, the school and even Ms Adolf are all taken from my life. I took the Broadway bus number 104 to school every day.

What was it like growing up with dyslexia?

When I was growing up in New York City, no one knew what dyslexia was. I was called stupid and lazy, and I was told that I was not living up to my potential. It was, without a doubt, painful. I spent most of my time covering up the fact that reading, writing, spelling, maths, science – actually, every subject but lunch – was really, really difficult for me. If I went to the shop and paid the bill with paper money and I was given coins back for change, I had no idea how to count up the change in my head. I just trusted that everyone was being honest.

What's it like working as a team to write the World's Greatest Underachiever books?

We have the most wonderful time working together. Lin sits at the computer, and I walk in a circle in front of her desk. If I start talking like the characters, Lin kindly types it in because I don't use a computer. Or, she'll tell me to stop for minute because she's got a great idea and her fingers fly across the keyboard. Sometimes, I'll write my chapters in long hand and Lin will transcribe them and correct my spelling. When the book is done, we both go over it to see if we've left anything out, or perhaps we'll find a better joke for one of the characters or better action in a scene. When it's completely done, we send it to our editor, and she sends back her notes that we then incorporate.

Did you always want to be an author?

Until the day that I met Lin Oliver for lunch in 2002, I never thought about being an author for one minute in my whole life.

How long does it take you to write a book?

It usually takes about two months to write the first draft of a book. Lin and I meet in her office and create the outline for the story of the book and then, two months later, we have a 153-page adventure about Hank Zipzer.

Which of your books do you like the best?

I cannot pick one book that I like the best. Each one of them is like my own child. Each one of them has some great detail that makes me laugh every time I think about it.